D1587467

DOCTOR · WHO

The Many Hands

DOCTOR·WHO

The
Many Hands

DALE SMITH

BBC
BOOKS

2 4 6 8 10 9 7 5 3 1

Published in 2008 by BBC Books, an imprint of Ebury Publishing.
Ebury Publishing is a division of the Random House Group Ltd.

© Dale Smith, 2008

Dale Smith has asserted his right to be identified as the author of this
Work in accordance with the Copyright, Design and Patents Act 1988.

Doctor Who is a BBC Wales production for BBC One
Executive Producers: Russell T Davies and Julie Gardner
Series Producer: Phil Collinson

Original series broadcast on BBC Television. Format © BBC 1963.
'Doctor Who', 'TARDIS' and the Doctor Who logo are trademarks of the
British Broadcasting Corporation and are used under licence.

The Random House Group Ltd Reg. No. 954009.
Addresses for companies within the Random House Group can be found
at www.randomhouse.co.uk.

A CIP catalogue record for this book is available from the British Library.

ISBN 978 1 84607 422 6

The Random House Group Limited supports the Forest Stewardship
Council (FSC), the leading international forest certification organisation.
All our titles that are printed on Greenpeace approved FSC certified
paper carry the FSC logo. Our paper procurement policy can be found
at www.rbooks.co.uk/environment

Series Consultant: Justin Richards
Project Editor: Steve Tribe
Cover design by Lee Binding © BBC 2008

Typeset in Albertina and Deviant Strain
Printed and bound in Germany by GGP Media GmbH, Poessneck

For the mother-in-law,
Ann Howkins

EDINBURGH, 1773

Katherine sat by the fire and sewed. The night was cold, and there would certainly be snow before the week was out. Her husband was out in the cold, somewhere. He was an academic. Katherine's mother had warned her about marrying a soldier, who would always be away fighting some war or another, but nothing had been said about academics. They, too, were often away, chasing down some elusive new truth, consulting with German colleagues about the minutiae of anatomy.

She had not seen Alexander in two days. She was not worried.

She sat by the fire and sewed.

'Katherine?' she heard him call.

She did not rise, nor did she answer. They had married eleven years earlier, four years after that they had taken this house. The city bustled outside day and night. A near never-ending stream of souls passing over the new North Bridge, each one desperate to make themselves heard over the trample of feet. They needed to be here, to be close to the University, for Alexander's work.

'Katherine?' he called again.

She did not rise, nor did she answer.

All the same, he found her. He appeared in the doorway, his clothing in some disarray, favouring his left leg as if his right was causing him pain. He looked at her, his sad tired eyes reminding her of why she had agreed to marry him, those eleven years ago. In his arms, he held a baby, wrapped in a woollen blanket. It didn't cry.

'Alexander!' she said, rising from her seat.

'I've been at the house,' he said, not moving from the doorway. That year, he had bought himself some two hundred acres in Craiglockhart, to indulge a passion for gardens. 'The child was left there, abandoned. He has no one to care for him, Katherine.'

Katherine was not one for simpering, but even she let out a gasp. She stroked the poor child's face with a finger: the flesh was ruddy and warm. Some God-given instinct made it hold her eye, recognising immediately the woman who was to be its mother, as if they had already long been acquainted. She took it from her husband and held it to her, and it did not cry.

'We shall need a wet-nurse,' Katherine said.

Her husband smiled, kindly.

'We will call him Alexander,' he announced.

'After yourself?' Katherine asked, eyebrow arched.

'It's an old family name,' her husband corrected.

EDINBURGH, 1759

ONE

It was a gloomy day in Edinburgh, but then when wasn't it? The city was almost constantly covered in a grey smudge of low lying cloud, always threatening to break rain. But the people of the city didn't let it put them off their business: the square throbbed with them, every inch of the Grassmarket filled with people hawking their wares, or preachers saving souls, or urchins picking the pockets of those foolish enough to stop. It couldn't have been busier if there was a hanging due.

In a moment, everything would change.

The screams washed down the crowd like a wave, causing each they touched to turn and stare. So packed was the square, it took a few moments before anybody could see anything. Then the crowd parted down the middle: men, women and children all fought to be away from the cobbled road and tried to climb the buildings that faced the square. Most didn't manage it, and some were felled simply by the weight of others trying to save themselves.

The air filled with a dreadful mix of clattering wheels and screaming horses. A small boy who was clinging to the wall of a public house rearranged his grip and strained to see. At the bend of the road he could see the stagecoach as it wove drunkenly towards them. The horses spat froth as they galloped blindly onwards, the driver clinging for his life to his perch and at the same time trying to pull the horses to a stop with the reins.

As the stagecoach raced by, the boy saw two men standing on its roof.

The Doctor crouched low as he tried to surf the stagecoach. The longer this went on, the more likely it was that people would get hurt: the driver was doing his best to steer the horses as they bolted, but it was a losing battle. Plus he couldn't fight the natural urge to look over his shoulder at his attacker; the pale man was having as much trouble as the Doctor in keeping his balance as the stagecoach rocked, but he was still advancing.

'Hey,' the Doctor called to the man.

The pale man didn't even turn, just kept shuffling cautiously towards the driver. He was wearing the muddy long-coat of a farmer, possibly a poacher, but as yet he hadn't reached for the knife that was tucked into his belt. Instead, his pale hands were outstretched, as if the only blades he needed were his own sharp fingernails. So far, the Doctor hadn't seen the man's face, just the lank strands of his hair flailing in the wind.

He tried a different tack.

'Entschuldigen?' he called.

The pale man turned, and the Doctor got a brief flash of black marble eyes and a triumphant feeling. Then he saw a piece of the stagecoach roof splinter, and looked again: the pale man's shoulder now had a dry red tear in it where something had struck him, attracting his attention.

The Doctor risked a glance behind him, and saw four red-jacketed soldiers firing from the steps down from the Castle.

'They're shooting at us!' cried a voice from below.

The Doctor ducked low to avoid perforation, and stuck his head out over the edge of the stagecoach. There was a passenger sticking his head out of the window and waving wildly.

'Don't worry,' the Doctor called as the coach veered violently to the left. 'Just stay inside.'

The passenger gave him a strange look, and ducked back inside.

The Doctor risked another look behind him, and saw the soldiers running after them whilst trying to reload their muskets. He was safe from that for a few moments, anyway. He pulled himself unsteadily to his feet and turned back to face forwards.

The pale man seemed to have lost interest in the driver, which was something. Instead, he was making shuffling steps towards the Doctor, those sharp little fingers outstretched.

Hold on a moment.

'Aren't you—' the Doctor started to shout to the passenger.

The stagecoach hit a loose cobble, and bucked into the air. The driver let out a cry and tried to keep hold of the reins and the coach and his wits, all in one messy manoeuvre. The coach tottered left, then teetered right, before deciding that perhaps it would remain on all four wheels for a few moments longer.

The Doctor, however, didn't have much time for relief: the pale man lost his footing as the coach kicked, and ended up diving for the Doctor, talons outstretched. Instead, he allowed himself a moment to wonder how Martha was doing.

Then the pale man knocked him on his back.

***

Martha ran.

As she ran, she kept her mind busy by listing the organisation of the human lung: the trachea, the bronchi, the bronchioles and the terminal bronchioles, the respiratory bronchioles, the alveolar ducts, and the alveoli. She remembered reading in one textbook that the alveoli had the same surface area as a tennis court. She counted off the diseases that affected the lungs, alphabetically. She kept getting stuck after oedema.

None of it would comfort her about the way her lungs burned.

Not five minutes ago, she had been standing on the ramparts of Edinburgh Castle enjoying the view. The Doctor had been talking, the way he did, about how she was seeing something no one else would ever see again. Clear countryside, all the way down to the Firth of Forth: Edinburgh before they built the bits of Edinburgh she remembered from that film. Then he'd told her why they'd needed to expand, turning to point down at the 80,000 people pushing their way through a daily life on the streets of the Old Town.

'Well,' the Doctor had said. 'Just "the Town" at the moment, but…'

Now here she was, pushing through it herself.

'Three,' she panted. 'Four. Seven.'

A woman dressed as a novelty toilet-roll cover

stepped out of her house to Martha's right, and nearly ended up flat on her bustle as Martha barged past. Martha didn't even look behind her, but she heard the decidedly ungentlemanly shouts coming from the lady's companion. They weren't the first to be annoyed by her: as she ran down the High Street, she had been knocking people left, right and centre. The houses that towered up three and four storeys on either side of the wide road were the town houses of the great and the good, and there hadn't been a single soul she had barged past that had had so much as a smudge of dust on their person. Until she'd sent them sprawling in the gutter.

On her right, she saw the archway. The sign above it announced it as Fishmarket Close, although it looked like it was just a tunnel that burrowed deep into the cellars of the houses. Martha turned sharply and ran into the darkness, the smell of fish rushing up to greet her as she ran. The ground sloped away from her feet at an alarming speed, and she knew that if she lost her footing for even a moment, she'd be tumbling. It took her a moment to realise that she had passed through the archway and was out in the fresh air again: as the ground dropped away, the tops of the houses remained on a level and the sunlight found it harder and harder to reach her.

The streets were even worse now she was off the

Royal Mile, filled with more people in worse clothes and splattered with a thick brown mud that she was starting to suspect wasn't actually mud. The houses seemed little more than tiny boxes, all piled high on top of each other like the estates in Tower Hamlets. Each had a metal spiral staircase outside it, leading up to the higher levels that looked barely big enough to let a child up comfortably. The language grew fouler as she bumped and barged, and more than one person started throwing things after her.

She had a momentary image of the houses on the Royal Mile as nothing more than a flimsy rubber mask, pulled aside to reveal the monstrous decay of the real city beneath...

Martha burst out of the street, and suddenly found herself blinking in the sunlight for a moment. She had never really pushed through a crowd of people running in the opposite direction before she'd met the Doctor. It wasn't something she particularly enjoyed. People were losing their footing and falling all around her, and the doctor in her wanted to stop and check they were all right. The Doctor in her made her keep moving, pushing and swerving into every space she was forcing open. The sound of their screaming was deafening. She wasn't going to make it, she knew.

'Three. Four. Seven,' she panted.

Suddenly the crowd thinned around her. At the

same time, their screams got louder as they realised the danger they were in was so much more imminent. They parted like water around her, eager to fill up the small space she had left them that much further from destruction. Another moment, and Martha was alone, standing gasping for breath in the middle of the cobbled road. She had to bend double just to force the air into her lungs.

'Run, girl!' someone shouted, but she didn't see who.

She stood up straight and composed herself.

As she turned, she saw the stagecoach careering down the road towards her, the driver having given up all pretence at control and just looking for the right moment to jump. She couldn't see the Doctor or the highwayman he'd been chasing. Perhaps they'd both fallen, and were lying broken further up the road. The streets were empty. After the press of the crowd, it felt more alien than any planet she'd set foot on.

The horses were heading straight for her, teeth bared.

She held up a hand, and didn't flinch.

'Three four seven,' she said.

In some ways, the Doctor supposed, it could be considered quite restful. OK, so he was in very real danger of getting a terminal haircut from the buildings lining the Cowgate, but at least he was lying down. And he had the wind blowing through his hair, an advantage that the stagecoach's bald driver was completely missing out on. All he needed was the certainty of being alive when the coach stopped, and it would be a very jolly afternoon's ride.

The pale man was kneeling over the Doctor, having seemingly no interest in picking himself up and resuming his attack on the driver. Nor was he attacking the Doctor, as such. Yes, he was flailing those sharp fingernails around, but if it was an attack it was a particularly unfocused one. An unbiased observer might be hard-pushed to decide if the nails were aimed at the Doctor, or merely trying to claw their way through the stagecoach roof. Certainly the pale man wasn't looking at him as the blows fell: he stared glassily into space, one pupil larger than the other. The Doctor filed the information in case it was important later.

The Doctor looked at the driver, who glanced back apologetically.

'Don't worry,' the Doctor shouted. 'I've got a friend.'

The stagecoach bounced again, and the Doctor's pale attacker rolled across the roof. For a moment, he looked as if he might fall, but at the last minute he twisted and somehow ended up back on his feet.

As the pale man rolled his glassy eyes in the Doctor's vague direction, a thin sliver of drool ran down his chin.

'I can help you,' the Doctor told him.

A musket shot rang out.

Martha swallowed hard, and closed her eyes.

'Three four seven,' she said.

The sonic screwdriver felt heavy in her hand, but she held it high. Her thumb found the switch without her having to look, and she pressed it down. She couldn't help flinching, even though she knew it wasn't going to explode in her hand. Probably wasn't going to explode in her hand. It wasn't making any sound, or at least none that she could hear. She risked a peek through one squinting eye.

The horses were nearly on top of her.

Her mouth fell open and her eyes opened wide. The stagecoach was hurtling towards her, the driver crossing himself and jumping from his perch to land awkwardly on the cobbles below. But she could see the highwayman and the Doctor, standing on the roof of the coach as if they were meeting in a bar for the first time. The Doctor was holding his hand out to the highwayman, saying something the clatter of hoof-beats was drowning out.

He was incredible.

There was the faint sound of a car backfiring that Martha barely noticed, until she remembered that this was a good couple of hundred years before internal combustion. The highwayman on the roof twitched and tumbled from the stagecoach roof. Martha barely had the time to register that he'd been shot before her heart leapt at the sight of the Doctor launching himself after him. The two met in mid-air, as the Doctor spun to protect the highwayman from the stone cobbles.

Just incredible.

Martha realised she was still standing in the path of the stagecoach.

It was too late, far too late. Martha could see those who had managed to get themselves out of the exact place she was standing looking back at her with a mixture of sympathy and excitement. This would be one to tell the grandchildren about, no doubt. All Martha could do was worry about whether the Doctor had hurt himself in the fall.

The horses let out a strange noise and slowed.

It was so odd to see: one moment, the horses were charging foam-mouthed towards her and she had no chance of survival; the next, they were starting to slow, flicking their manes about as if they were in an equine shampoo advert. Martha felt a moment of elation, before she realised that the stagecoach itself wasn't slowing down.

As the horses both moved to the left, suddenly interested in the buildings lining the street, the stagecoach sped on at top speed. The gathered crowd didn't know what to do, and neither did the horses. They dug their feet in indignantly as the coach pulled them backwards down the road, their hooves grinding sparks from the rough stone.

Martha let her hand drop and made a run for the dubious protection of a pub. She felt a rush of wind try to pull her jacket from her back, but didn't stop. As she jumped, she ended up clutching the hand of a young, red-haired boy, who was himself hanging precariously from the jacket of a heavy-set man who didn't look much like he wanted to be hung from. Other hands came down to sweep her up, and for a moment she let herself fall into them. It felt like having her mother hug her after a nasty tumble.

When she looked behind her, the stagecoach had spun to a halt ten yards down the road. The cobblestones were scuffed, and the coach was sideways on to the road, but otherwise you'd be hard pushed to guess that anything was wrong. The horses pawed at the ground skittishly, and tried hard not to catch each other's eye. Martha had the strangest feeling that they were embarrassed. She smiled, and took her thumb from the sonic screwdriver.

***

The Doctor rolled.

It wasn't something he'd been planning to do, but when it came down to it he didn't seem to have much choice in the matter, and it seemed churlish to fight it. Everybody needed a good roll every now and again. Somewhere along the way, he'd got separated from the pale man he'd been trying to save, but at least it saved him the trouble of trying to calculate exactly what the man's ambient skin temperature was. Certainly two degrees below the human norm, but was it two point one or not?

Then he stopped. All good things come to an end.

He lay on his back for just a moment, enjoying the feel of the hard cobbles against his back, admiring the dramatic beauty of the monochrome clouds directly above. Gradually the sound of the crowd filtered into his perception, and he made a rough estimate of how long it would take before one of them rushed over and asked if he was all right. He ought to save them the bother and leap to his feet, but just for the moment his body seemed to want a nice lie-down.

He managed to lift his head a little.

The soldiers were coming.

The Doctor sighed.

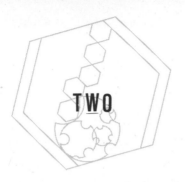

TWO

Martha rushed over to where the Doctor was lying, kneeling on the ground by his side and starting to sweep her hands down his body, checking for broken bones. There was nothing leaking out of his ears, so he might have survived a fractured skull. Somehow, she didn't think there was going to be much opportunity for an X-ray and a lie-down with a nice bunch of grapes.

The Doctor's eyes snapped open, and he grinned at her.

She couldn't help grinning back.

'Are you OK?' she asked. 'Do you know what year it is?'

'1759,' the Doctor answered.

For just a moment, Martha thought he must

have suffered some kind of concussion. Then she remembered.

'Check on our friend,' the Doctor ordered, bouncing to his feet. The Doctor nodded, and Martha turned. 'I'll make the introductions.'

Four soldiers were rushing down the street, with a fifth marching briskly behind them. He had bristling black hair and dark little eyes that flicked this way and that as he marched. Martha didn't know anything about military insignia, but she recognised that the man was in charge from the look of distaste as he watched the others running.

'Go!' urged the Doctor.

He pushed her away, towards the body lying just a few feet from where the horses were snorting and patting the ground. She'd forgotten all about the other man, just for a moment. The Doctor had taken priority. She tried not to blush as she hurried over.

The man wasn't moving, lying face down on the cobblestones with his limbs splayed out around him. Without even touching him, Martha could tell that the left arm was broken, the ulna and the radius hopefully snapped clean and not greenstick. It stuck out at an unnatural angle, the flesh below the break even paler than the rest. If she was back at the Royal Hope, it would be simple to reset the bones. Here she wasn't sure if she could save the arm.

'Hello,' she said as she knelt. 'My name's Martha: I'm a doctor. Can you hear me?'

The patient didn't answer her. Was he unconscious?

The temptation to get to work on the arm was a strong one, but it was wrong too. She had done her rotation in the A&E department like everyone else, and had been told the stories of the patients wheeled in with perfectly bandaged broken arms. Dead on arrival, because the first people on the scene had forgotten to check the patient was breathing before they got out the bandages.

ABC, Martha told herself.

Airway, Breathing, Circulation. Then the arm.

She knelt down with her hand next to the patient's mouth and nose, but couldn't feel the comforting rush of air from his lungs. She pressed her fingers against his jugular, but couldn't feel the swell of pumping blood. If she turned him and he'd damaged his spine, she could paralyse him. She'd definitely make the arm worse. If she didn't turn him, then he would die. There was no contest.

She rolled him sharply onto his back, and saw…

'Oh!'

The Doctor strolled over to the soldiers as breezily as he could manage having just jumped from a speeding stagecoach. All things considered, he thought he managed it quite well: he kept smiling the whole time, to suggest to the soldiers that the idea of them thinking him a threat hadn't even crossed his mind. Their captain studiously ignored him, continuing his steady march onwards until he reached the coach's driver and could bully the man to his feet. The four soldiers, on the other hand, stopped about two feet from the Doctor and raised their muskets.

The Doctor smiled broadly, as if they'd offered him tea.

'Hello,' he grinned, slipping easily into a gentle Scots burr. 'I'm the Doctor, and that's my friend Martha Jones.'

'What are you doing?' Martha asked him.

He gave the soldiers another smile, and looked awkwardly over his shoulder. Martha was standing behind him, her arms folded across her chest. It occurred to him that he probably should have thanked her for stopping the horses.

'Blending in,' he stage-whispered in his natural Southern twang.

'In that coat?'

The Doctor looked down at his long coat, his bottom lip sticking out like a small, sulky child. There was nothing wrong with the coat – it certainly fitted better in the eighteenth century than it did in the twenty-fifth: all that tinfoil clothing and heavy eye make-up. He looked back up at Martha.

'He's dead,' she said.

Another failure.

'I'm sorry,' he told her.

But she was shaking her head.

'No, I mean he's dead,' she repeated. 'Really dead: he's got an autopsy scar and everything.'

The Doctor blinked. He threw a quick look over his shoulder: the Captain was talking to the stagecoach's passengers, and the soldiers were giving him that look which said they weren't quite sure what to do now that their weapons hadn't got them the attention they were used to.

He gave them an apologetic smile and turned back to Martha. He held out his hand, and she dropped the sonic screwdriver into it with a smile.

'Well, I'd better take a look then,' he announced.

As soon as the sonic screwdriver was in the Doctor's hand, Martha knew everything was going to be all right. The glasses came out of his jacket pocket, and then he squinted over them at whatever the screwdriver was telling him. Only the Doctor would put on glasses he probably didn't need to treat a screwdriver like an MRI scanner. She looked at the soldiers with a smile and shrugged.

'Hmm,' the Doctor said, pushing his glasses further up his nose.

'Well?' Martha asked.

He looked at her and frowned. 'He's dead. Has been for two days at least. Brain haemorrhage: that explains the blown pupil. There's all sorts of funny energy floating about in there, but…'

Martha looked at him with a raised eyebrow.

'And you can tell all that with a screwdriver?' she said.

'A *sonic* screwdriver – Hey!'

Martha jumped as the Doctor tore his glasses off and stormed across the road, waving them angrily around. She spun around as fast as she could – noticing with a smile that their armed guard was equally surprised – and saw the stagecoach pulling away. The driver gave the Doctor a brief glance over his shoulder, and then gave the whip a crack. The horses changed gear from canter to gallop and, by the time the Doctor reached the head soldier, the stagecoach had turned to the right and disappeared.

'What did you do that for?' the Doctor shouted.

Martha hurried over to join him, followed closely by four soldiers. Their leader merely stood and let his hands meet behind his back, perfectly at ease. He looked at the Doctor with two dark eyes that glinted underneath thin little eyebrows.

'The journey to London takes two weeks,' the soldier said, chewing the words as if they tasted off. His accent, surprisingly, was English. 'I don't think there needs to be any further delay, do you?'

'They might have been able to tell us something about the attack,' Martha jumped in.

The head soldier gave her a dismissive look.

'I questioned the driver and his passenger,' he said, just a little snootily. 'I'm satisfied they have nothing further to add.'

'Yes, but,' said the Doctor, waving a stern finger. 'Captain…?'

'McAllister,' the soldier said. He gave a little snort to show how surprised he was that there was a man in the world that didn't automatically know his name. 'And you are?'

'He's the Doctor,' Martha said. She smiled sweetly, as her mother had told her to when dealing with idiots. 'I'm Martha Jones.'

'Well, Doctor, Miss Jones,' McAllister said silkily. 'You're under arrest. Get them to the Tolbooth.'

The soldiers took a step forward, but the Doctor already had his psychic paper in his hand.

'Now I don't think His Majesty would appreciate that,' he said casually. 'And I really would've liked to speak to that passenger.'

McAllister read the paper and raised an eyebrow.

'And why would that be?' he asked.

The Doctor grinned infectiously. 'Well,' he said. 'That kite thing was brilliant!'

Martha looked at the Doctor for a moment, and not for the first time wondered what he was on about. Captain McAllister seemed to be in on the secret, though, as his thin moustache twitched a little. He didn't return the Doctor's smile.

'So you knew who was travelling in the coach?'

'I think I must have seen his photograph in *Heat*,' the Doctor answered solemnly, with a twinkle in his eye. 'I do read it rather a lot, don't I, Martha?'

Martha just grinned.

'And that would be why you attempted to ambush the stagecoach, yes?' McAllister said.

The Doctor's face fell and he glanced from the Captain to Martha and back again. The Captain simply stood, his hands behind his back, breathing softly through his mouth.

'Oh no! We weren't trying to ambush the stagecoach. You see my friend and I were standing in the Castle admiring the view—'

'*And* you were trespassing in the Castle.'

'This was a different castle. We saw that dead man over there jump onto the roof of the stagecoach, and the horses panicked – probably because he'd been dead for two days and—'

The Doctor turned to Martha. She folded her arms.

'He's not going to believe that, is he?'

Martha shook her head.

'I don't care who you reckon you are: you're going to the Tolbooth. Brown, stop scratching MacDonald's backside and step to it!' Captain McAllister suddenly yelled. The four soldiers jumped visibly. 'Connolly, get that corpse up to the Castle and send a runner to tell the surgeons where they can find it. Perhaps it won't be so difficult to guard a man who's already dead.'

Martha saw the hint of a smile pull at the Captain's mouth: clearly he was pleased at the thought and wit he'd managed to put into his orders. One of the soldiers shouldered his musket and set his face with a grim look as he headed over to the pale corpse, hefting it up over his shoulder. The other soldiers each pointed their muskets at Martha and the Doctor.

'What about me?' Martha asked, pushing up to the Captain. 'I wasn't attacking the coach: I stopped it. You can't arrest me for that.'

The gathered crowd murmured something to each other that might have been agreement, or equally disappointment that the show was apparently coming to a natural end. All the same, Martha gave the Captain the same look she would have if the crowd had all spontaneously cheered and carried her around the market on its shoulders. If she could stay out of prison, she'd have a much better chance of being able to help the Doctor.

Captain McAllister looked her up and down.

'You are wearing pantaloons,' he said pointedly.

Martha looked down at herself, and realised that he was talking about her jeans. She almost laughed out loud, despite the funny look on the Doctor's face.

'What, and that's against the law is it?'

'Ah, actually it is,' the Doctor muttered into her ear. 'For women. Sorry.'

Martha looked from the Doctor to the frowning soldier. Right, OK – so she was actually going to be arrested for crimes against fashion. Tish was right after all.

Martha crooked her arm at the Doctor.

'Doctor?' she said.

'Miss Jones,' the Doctor agreed.

And they walked back up the slope of Fishmarket Close towards the Royal Mile, arm in arm.

THREE

The soldiers kept near as they trudged back up the lethal slope to the Royal Mile – one of the three pacing in front, whilst the other marched behind under the watchful glare of Captain McAllister. The street hadn't become any less busy in the last few minutes, but Martha found going up a lot easier than coming down. The presence of the soldiers created a bubble around her and the Doctor: people paused on the edge of the Close as they were marched by, and then carried on as normal.

It reminded Martha oddly of a royal parade, but one that was taking in the less scenic areas of the city and was dogged by the pungent odour of fish wherever it went. Every now and again, someone who hadn't seen the stagecoach drama would cross their path and stop in wonderment. As they were pulled out of the way by a throng of clutching hands, the sound of voices increased as everybody in the crowd tried to tell the newcomer the news.

Martha clung on tight to the Doctor. He smiled at the crowds cheerfully.

'So who was in the stagecoach?' Martha hissed.

'Only one of this century's most brilliant minds,' the Doctor said. He didn't seem to care if the soldiers overheard. Captain McAllister seemed content to divide his time between belittling his men and giving Martha evil looks, occasionally growling warningly at the people who got in his way. 'You should know him: he invented bi-focal spectacles. And the catheter.'

'Right,' Martha said. 'I think I met him at a party once.'

'You don't know?' the Doctor asked, shocked.

'No!' Martha laughed.

'Quiet!' Captain McAllister barked behind them.

'What did they teach you in that teaching hospital?' the Doctor grumbled, completely ignoring McAllister.

'Oh you know,' Martha whispered. She wasn't quite as certain as the Doctor that the Captain wouldn't order his men to open fire just for some peace and quiet. 'They just wasted time teaching us things like how to save lives and ease human suffering.'

'Appalling!' the Doctor cried.

But he smiled that smile, and Martha couldn't help returning it. No matter what it did to Captain McAllister's mood.

'So who was it?' Martha asked again.

'Benjamin Franklin,' the Doctor answered.

Martha snorted.

'All right, don't tell me then.'

'I did,' the Doctor protested. 'It was!'

'Benjamin Franklin invented the catheter? You're kidding.'

The Doctor shook his head, the picture of wide-eyed innocence.

'What would he be doing in Scotland anyway?' she asked.

'Well,' the Doctor said, scratching the side of his nose with a finger. 'In 1759... I suppose he'd be picking up his honorary degree from St Andrews University. It's not far from here as the crow flies, and it took him two weeks to get here: he'd want to do a bit of sightseeing.'

'Two weeks to get here from America?'

'Oh no,' the Doctor said. 'It's two weeks to get here from London. You're probably talking at least two months to get here from America.'

'They must be counting the days before someone invents Travel Scrabble,' Martha said.

The Doctor smiled.

'Benjamin Franklin's living in London now,' the Doctor explained. 'That's another thing he did: diplomacy. He's the Pennsylvania Assembly's agent to the Government of the United Kingdom of Great Britain and Ireland.'

'Pennsylvania's?' Martha shook her head. 'Did the Cotswolds get to send an agent to America as well?'

'Ye-es,' said the Doctor, extending the word out as long as it would go without breaking. 'Don't forget, the Americas are just a collection of separate colonies at the moment. They don't unite for another sixteen years, when they fight the… Well, before that thing that unites them.'

'You mean the…' Martha said slowly, looking nervously at the two loaded muskets pointing her way.

'That's the one,' the Doctor agreed in a whisper. 'But that's just the sort of talk that makes British soldiers nervous, so there's no reason why we need to throw words like "American revolution" around, is there?'

'Oh no,' Martha agreed. 'No reason at all.'

And she smiled at the soldiers.

They didn't smile back.

'Halt,' McAllister yelled.

His voice echoed through the air for a moment.

They had emerged out of the passageway and back onto the High Street, making the return considerably more slowly than Martha had made her descent. The soldier in front, a grey-haired man who she thought was the one McAllister had called Brown, was panting audibly. She didn't dare think what he would have been like if McAllister had chosen him to carry the highwayman's body back to the Castle: that soldier had disappeared up the Cowgate at a gallop, muttering pityingly to himself about the stairs he would have to climb at the end of it.

Without pause, McAllister had turned them to the left and marched them back up the sloping street, the old soldier taking the opportunity to duck behind them and slacken his pace. As they moved, more people gathered on the edges of the street to watch, but the reaction was different here. The street was wider, so Martha wasn't brushing through the crowd, but she had the feeling that these people weren't as nervous of the soldiers. After all, the army was on their side, protecting them from the criminal tendencies of the poor below the hill.

It didn't take long to reach their destination: they stopped in a large square, in front of an imposing church. It seemed to be made exclusively from giant slabs of stone and dark serrated towers stabbing up into the air, the product of a time when believers were reminded God should be feared, as well as loved. Attached to the church, and blocking off the square from the Lawnmarket, was a large building four storeys tall with a tower running down the front of it, reminding Martha of the Castle that sat at the top of the hill.

'That's the Tolbooth,' the Doctor whispered to her.

'I suppose it's not the kind I'll need change for?' Martha whispered in reply.

'It's an old Scots word,' the Doctor answered softly. 'It's where the council meets.'

'Well,' said Martha with enforced cheerfulness. 'That doesn't sound so bad.'

'And they usually have prisons underneath them.'

'Oh,' said Martha.

McAllister studiously ignored his prisoners, choosing instead to glare at the three red-coated men.

'You three get the prisoners to the cells,' McAllister instructed sharply. 'I'll be talking with the Lord Provost, and if I have to be called out because of any of you…'

The threat hung in the air for a moment, then McAllister marched inside.

There was a moment in which the soldiers relaxed slightly, their shoulders drooping as the tension created by McAllister's presence eased. Despite all the years between them, Martha could recognise her old colleagues in the soldiers: if they'd been back at the hospital, the soldiers would have been junior doctors leaning against the wall and starting to gossip the moment the consultant's back was turned. Sometimes, she wished she was back with them: since she'd met the Doctor, there never seemed to be any time to relax. They'd been in Edinburgh not even an hour, and already he'd had her running up and down hills and diving in front of stagecoaches – it was better than any gym, at least.

It was only when they got thrown into prison that she got any chance to rest, these days.

Martha could see that the Doctor was already tensing. He seemed to have an inbuilt aversion to authority: it would never occur to him, for example, to speak to the Lord Provost himself and explain the situation. That there was something abroad in Edinburgh that had brought the dead to life, and if it had done it once, it might easily do it again. No, the Doctor would want to be out there himself, chasing down the solution on his own. And that meant escaping from soldiers and prisons whenever he got the chance, and legs like Paula Radcliffe for her.

The Doctor took her hand, and waggled his eyebrows.

They ran.

She looked behind and saw that the soldiers had been just as surprised as she had. Two of them fumbled with their muskets, one landing on the cobbled street with a loud clatter that convinced some pedestrians that it had gone off. The third, however, was a little quicker than his friends and was already chasing after them. Perhaps he was the one who feared the Captain's reaction the most.

'Where are we going?' Martha shouted to the Doctor.

He was, annoyingly, two paces ahead of her and holding her arm in a way that suggested he could be six if he wasn't. He threw her a smile, which she gratefully caught.

'This way,' he said.

Instead of pulling her down the road to their left that must have led back down to the Grassmarket, he pulled her upwards, towards the Castle. She couldn't help thinking that there had to be a better place to run, but it was too late to argue.

There was a crack of musket fire.

The Doctor pulled on Martha's arm again.

When she saw where he was heading, she tried to pull away.

Even the Doctor couldn't think that was a good idea.

***

John Connolly shouldered his musket as he ran. He'd had his one shot and, if he stopped to reload now, he'd lose them. Mac and Gordy were close on his heels but, as good lads as they were, John wouldn't trust them to find the cludgie before they wet themselves. If the prisoners had it away, McAllister would have them all scraping out the latrines with their fingernails and licking them clean before dinner.

He stayed a breath behind the strangely dressed pair as they ran up Castle Hill: he expected they'd try to disappear down one of the Closes and out of the city that way. Once they were out in the open, he could risk a few moments to reload and wing them. He should be able to make the shot. He practically had his musket in his hands when he saw them turn the other way instead. Were they soft in the head? They were running straight into the Castle: once they were inside, where would they expect to go?

'We've got them now!' Mac shouted.

Gordy didn't say a word: he had a good few years on Mac and John, and his prime running days were long behind him. He was already panting hard, the poor old'un.

As they came out onto the brow of the hill, the Castle loomed up over them: it looked more like a mansion than anything John would have called a castle, but the giant plug of rock it sat on had kept the enemy at bay since Adam and Eve's time. The ground before the Castle was just a wide, empty expanse with little place to hide. Any approaching army would have to march unprotected before they reached the narrow archway at the far side offering entry into the main Castle. It was a system that had served them well those fourteen years back when the Pretender's men had taken Edinburgh, but not the Castle. The gates remained firmly closed now as well, just in case the Jacobite ghost hadn't been properly laid to rest after all.

At any other time, there might perhaps have been a brigade of redcoats practising their drill to lose yourself amongst, but right now the Castle had only a handful of city guards to call on, and the ground was empty. All the same, John had expected the prisoners to at least try: instead, they were just standing there, waiting to be recaptured. The man was standing straight watching them approach with a grim look. The woman was bent double trying to catch her breath, but her eyes were locked on the three redcoats from the moment they appeared. The look on her face said that she had expected to be hiding as well. She tried to pull away from the man as John moved up, but he held her tight to him.

Poor girl: if it came to shooting, John thought he'd try to get her clean.

John, Mac and Gordy all looked at each other,

and slowed to a trot. John took his musket from his shoulder as he went: he still hadn't loaded it, but the prisoners weren't to know that. Besides, Mac and Gordy were holding theirs too, pointing them meaningfully at the man and his woman.

'What're they doing?' hissed Mac.

John had to shrug.

'Don't come any closer!' the man shouted.

John stopped, involuntarily. The man was holding the leather wallet with the paper in that he'd shown to the Captain. It hadn't cut much ice at the bottom of the hill, and John was pretty sure the prisoner couldn't expect things to be any different up here.

'You're to come wi' us to the Tolbooth,' John announced loudly, raising his musket meaningfully. 'The Captain don't care who you are. Neither do we.'

The man smiled again.

'Ah,' he said, gently shaking his head. 'But that was down there. Now I'm standing here – absolutely right here – I think your Captain will care very much. You see, this says I'm Baronet Jones of Nova Scotia, and you are trespassing on my land. If you try to step one inch closer, it will be considered an act of war.'

John and Mac looked at each other.

The woman looked at them apologetically.

'So go on,' the man said. 'Off you go.'

They raised their muskets.

FOUR

Martha stood, fighting for her breath next to the Doctor. He just stood ramrod straight, holding his psychic paper with one hand, and Martha's hand with the other. With her back to the Castle at the top of the hill, she had a perfect view of the city, all the way back down the full mile of road to Holyrood Palace at the foot of the hill. She could even make out the deep blue of the Firth of Forth out there, and catch the odd glimpse of the extinct volcano called Arthur's Seat between the houses. She could see why the King or Queen that owned the Castle had built it: it was a beautiful view, even if it would be the last she ever saw.

She saw the soldiers raise their muskets and instinct told her to blink, as if her eyelids would stop the bullets in their tracks. She didn't though: if the Doctor felt safe enough to face the bullets down, then so did she.

Even if the Doctor was clearly insane.

'Hold on,' said the grey-haired soldier, between pants. 'He's right.'

Martha looked up at the Doctor in disbelief, but he was watching the soldiers with that insane smile of his spread all over his face. There was no way this was going to work. No way.

'What d'you mean he's right?' one of the younger soldiers snapped.

The muskets were still pointing at the Doctor and Martha.

'He's right,' said the old, panting man. 'They made part of the grounds the territory of Nova Scotia for the sasine. And they're standing on it.'

'Oh, come on, Gordy!' shouted the other soldier.

Martha leant in close to the Doctor. 'What's sasine?' she asked.

'It's part of the ceremony where they make you a baronet.' The Doctor answered. He didn't take his eyes off the soldiers' muskets, but still he grinned like the Cheshire Cat that got the cream. 'They give you the land you've been made baronet of – the sasine. Except the Scots take it a little more literally here: they really give you the land. But Nova Scotia is part of Canada.'

'Two months away,' Martha said, remembering.

'So it's much less trouble to make part of Old Scotia a little piece of Nova Scotia, rather than sail to the other side of the planet to pick up some dirt every time you need to make someone a baronet.'

'And you just happened to know which bit to stand on?'

The Doctor looked a little hurt.

'I am *really* a baronet,' he protested.

'Of Nova Scotia?'

'Bathgate,' he answered. 'But still…'

'Let's just shoot them,' one of the soldiers said, raising his musket.

Martha looked at them, expecting the older soldier to repeat that the Doctor was right, that he had the power to order them away. He didn't. Instead he looked at them with sad grey eyes and looked like he'd much rather be somewhere else whilst somebody else took the decision for him. Martha opened her mouth, but the Doctor laid a warning hand on her arm.

'There's no need for any trouble,' he said, fixing the older soldier with a look. 'You're just ordinary soldiers: nobody's expecting you to know about things like this. But if you get it wrong you'll be in all sorts of trouble. There's not really a lot you can do, is there?'

It sounded so reasonable the way he said it, Martha

half-expected them to lay down their muskets and surrender right there. Instead, the youngest of the soldiers had a brainwave.

'Gordy,' he said to the old soldier. 'You go back to the Tolbooth and get McAllister. He's the high heid yin: let him have the trouble.'

'Oh there's no need for that,' the Doctor said, a little too fast. 'We can—'

'Gordy!' the youngster snapped. 'You go now.'

Gordy stood for a moment, wracked by indecision. Martha could see it on his face, and the pair of them could see that the youngster had his own particular solution to the problem in mind. They both knew that if Captain McAllister had wanted them dead, he could have easily said so… but equally, they could see that the young soldier had made his mind up. And anything he did now would be his doing and his doing alone: McAllister wouldn't have any call to spread the blame around.

'Aye, Mac,' Gordy said, letting his head fall. 'I'll fetch McAllister.'

He didn't look at Martha as he ran back down to the Tolbooth. Probably his conscience wouldn't allow it.

The Doctor let out a satisfied sigh. 'Good,' he said. 'Now it's just the four of us.'

The two soldiers looked at each other nervously, and kept their muskets high. The Doctor didn't even seem to notice, and took a step forward, smiling disarmingly. Not disarmingly enough: the muskets were still pointing at him. Martha did her best to keep a positive attitude, but an image of the Doctor lying on the ground with a few extra holes in him kept flashing into her mind's eye.

'Doctor...' she said warningly as he took another step.

'Don't worry,' the Doctor said, a hand sliding slowly into his jacket's inside pocket. 'There's only two of them now, and I haven't shown you everything this can do yet.'

In his hand, the sonic screwdriver glinted briefly.

The two soldiers looked at each other again, as if trying to decide if the small wand was some kind of weapon. Or perhaps they were deciding between them if the Doctor was a witch, and this was his magic wand. They both tensed and moved their fingers towards the triggers. As they took their eyes off him, the Doctor moved forwards again. Now the musket barrels were pressing against his chest. Each heart would get its own bullet.

'Doctor...' Martha said again.

The Doctor's hand moved.

Martha flinched, expecting both the crack of gunfire and the sonic screwdriver to do something strange and terrible. Neither happened: the Doctor didn't even move to turn the screwdriver on. Instead, he flicked it, rapping the younger soldier firmly between the eyes with the blue-bulbed end. The young soldier was so startled that he dropped his musket and immediately began rubbing his head. As he did, the Doctor stamped hard on the other's toes. The soldier's musket clattered to the floor as he let out a cry and started hopping up and down.

The Doctor performed a quick bow, during which he scooped the two fallen muskets up into his arms and spun to face Martha.

'Shall we run?' he asked politely.

Martha let out a laugh, and ran.

'I can't believe you got away with that,' Martha laughed as she ran.

If he was entirely honest, neither could the Doctor.

'It's 1759,' he said by way of explanation. 'Scotland's been dragged into the Seven Years War because of the Act of Union: all the best soldiers are over in Europe fighting the French. The ones that are left behind... well, have you ever watched *Dad's Army*?'

'Doctor,' said Martha. She pointed down the side of the hill, where a red-coated soldier was manoeuvring a dead body onto the back of a cart before covering it with a thick, oiled tarpaulin.

The Doctor couldn't see much of the body before it

was covered, but he thought it was a good bet that it was their miraculous autopsy-surviving, stagecoach-hijacking friend.

'All right,' the Doctor said, rubbing his hands together. 'Who fancies hitching a ride to the Surgeon's Hall?'

'I'm not sure we'd make it very far,' Martha said, pointing again.

The Doctor looked back down Castle Hill. Down where the road turned into the Lawnmarket, he could see a knot of red jackets racing up towards them. The Doctor could practically hear Captain McAllister throwing out inspirational barbs to keep the men moving. Behind them, he could hear the two guards he'd embarrassed starting to gather their wits: if the two groups of soldiers met without the Doctor and Martha between them, they'd search in every house, under every tarpaulin, until they found them.

'OK,' the Doctor said, thinking fast. His eyes wandered to the north, and the volcanic rocks falling away to the Loch below. 'Here's what we do. I'll examine the body and see if I can work out why he was up and about this morning. You distract the soldiers: if you go that way, you can lose them on the side of the hill and double back to the Surgeon's Hall. There's a secret path there I'm sure they'll have forgotten about: Thomas Randolph used it in 1314 to retake the Castle from the English…'

The Doctor tailed off as he saw the look Martha was giving him.

'You don't know who Thomas Randolph was, do you?' he said.

Martha shook her head.

'And you don't know where the secret path is?'

'Actually,' Martha said, trying to hide a smile, 'I don't know where the Surgeon's Hall is either.'

The Doctor rubbed his eyes. He needed to see that body again, but there was no time. Why was he always living his life at such a frenetic pace, forever running out of time when he was supposed to be a Time Lord? Wouldn't it be nice to spend a couple of hours just immersing himself in the atmosphere?

'Right!' he cried, pointing at Martha. '*You* stay with the body. *I'll* lead the soldiers away. But the next time we're in the twenty-first century, I'm going to have a good long talk with your tutors about their curriculum.'

Martha smiled, and then she was gone.

The two young soldiers appeared behind him, and the Doctor spun with a look of guilty surprise on his face. Nine hundred years old, and he'd still make a pretty good Hamlet.

The Doctor pointed to the north as Martha ran to the south.

'Don't stop, Martha!' he yelled, introducing a note of panic to his voice. 'I'm right behind you.'

And then he ran.

Thankfully, the soldiers quickly gave chase.

Martha heard the Doctor shout, but didn't turn. Luckily, the soldier didn't seem to have noticed: he was round the other side, securing the tarpaulin over the back of the cart. Martha crept up to the side of the vehicle and tried to keep the wheels between him and her. As the soldier moved round to the front to pat the horse patiently standing there, Martha snuck round to the back and lifted the tarpaulin.

There was a smell that made her wrinkle her nose.

The body in the back was definitely the man from the stagecoach: his shirt and trousers were battered and ripped from when he'd fallen from the roof, and Martha could make out the vivid red of the autopsy scar down his bare chest. He wasn't the first body she had seen, but he was the first that she was planning on lying down next to and somehow she thought she owed him some kind of apology for that.

'Sorry,' she whispered as she clambered up onto the cart.

She slid under the tarpaulin, inching up beside the body slowly, trying not to make any sudden wriggles that the soldier might spot. The tarpaulin felt heavy, and didn't let any light under it. The smell was almost overpowering, but she knew that the soldier would hear if she made a sound. Then she would be caught, and the Edinburgh surgeons would do whatever they did to bodies in the eighteenth century, and the Doctor wouldn't be able to do whatever he wanted to do to this particular body from the eighteenth century. All the same, it was hard not to gag.

She closed her eyes and told herself how useful all this would be if she had to take any history of medicine exams when she got back home. Her leg started to itch, but there was nothing she could do. She'd have to just think about something else. Like the possibility that the itch was a fleabite: how common was the Bubonic Plague in the eighteenth century?

'Yar!' shouted the soldier, and the cart jolted forwards.

The body jolted too.

Martha ended up hugging it most of the way there.

FIVE

The Doctor moved as fast as he dared, leaping down the grassy slope of Castle Hill with all the abandon of a mountain goat, but one that liked to stop and enjoy the views every now and again. The soldiers were coming down behind him, but much less sure-footedly: it was a delicate dance between them, making sure they didn't get close enough to shoot him but didn't get so far behind that they lost him and started searching around the Castle again.

To make things more complicated, he didn't want to go so fast that his pursuers lost their footing and fell down the side of the hill. OK, so it wasn't Mount Everest, but it was still a good drop to the bottom, and even if they didn't break anything on the way down they'd probably catch dysentery if they landed in the water below. Edinburgh might be in the middle of its Enlightenment, but it still hadn't invented the sewer system yet. Unless you counted throwing it out the window and letting the rain wash it into the Loch as a 'system'.

He'd give Martha a couple more minutes, and then he'd find Randolph's path and disappear. Over in Ayrshire, Rabbie Burns had just been born: if he'd been a little older, he might have been able to tell the Doctor what happened to the best laid plans of mice and men…

A musket cracked off a shot behind him.

It was a foolish attempt, and any good soldier would have known it: the Doctor was too far away and too skittish to hit. But, as he'd told Martha, good soldiers were in short supply at the moment, and one of the not-so-good ones thought he could make the shot. At least he'd had the sense to stop running so he could aim, for all the good it did as the musketball thudded into the stone a few feet behind the Doctor.

The stone shattered, and shrapnel flew into the air.

One of the soldiers was caught in the face by it.

He let out a cry that mingled with the sharp bark of Captain McAllister, calling the gunman a selection of choice words. The injured soldier threw his hands up to his face, but he didn't stop running: he tripped over his own feet and went tumbling down the side of

Castle Hill, towards the Nor' Loch and its foul waters below.

'Of course,' the Doctor thought to himself, 'I could always keep going.'

He altered his course without slowing, charging down the side of the hill himself at a speed almost impossible to check. Large chunks of volcanic rock seemed to throw themselves under his feet, and he'd use them as springboards to launch himself away even faster. Two hundred years later, he told himself, and there would be a nice gentle footpath going down here. And a fairground waiting for him at the bottom.

'Fire!' McAllister shouted, letting the Doctor know he'd strayed within range of the muskets.

They missed. He'd have some time while they reloaded.

The soldier was still tumbling, no longer struggling to try to stop his fall: now he just fell limply, either resigned to his fate or knocked unconscious by a glancing blow from the old volcano. The Doctor hoped he was still conscious: he'd do himself less damage if he fell limp, but a blow that made him insensible could easily do so permanently.

'Hold on,' he shouted, and launched himself again.

The Doctor dived, cutting across the path of the falling soldier and grabbing him like he was a long-lost love. Arms wrapped tight around each other, the two began to roll sideways across the hill, all downward motion halted by the force of the Doctor's impact. For a few more moments, they rolled, and then the Doctor spread out his legs and an arm and suddenly he was lying on his back on the grass. The soldier was lying across his chest, his head face down on the ground.

For a moment, the Doctor admired the clouds again.

'Can you hear me?' the Doctor asked.

The soldier let out a little whimper.

'It's all right,' the Doctor said softly. 'You're going to be all right.'

Gently, the Doctor slid himself out from under the soldier. He held the boy's head as he rolled him onto his back. He was little more than sixteen. There were streaks of blood rolling down his face, and tiny stone chips imbedded in the flesh of his forehead. His eyes were screwed tight shut, and he was clutching his arm. The Doctor didn't have to look long to see that it was broken.

'What's your name?' he asked. 'I'm the Doctor.'

'Craig,' the boy grunted.

'All right, Craig,' the Doctor said. 'I'm just going to look at your eyes.'

The Doctor carefully lifted each eyelid in turn: no

damage from flying shrapnel. The arm was broken, but it would mend. It could have been a lot worse: he could have broken his back, or his neck, or his skull.

'All right, then,' the Doctor said, and then stopped.

'Don't move,' McAllister ordered.

Ten soldiers stood behind him on the hill.

Each had a musket trained on the Doctor.

McAllister looked down on his prisoner, and sneered. He was dressed like a traveller, his long coat being able to hide any number of things. His hair was too short, and that grin that he affected was decidedly manic. But he wasn't grinning now. No, he was glaring at McAllister as if he had ten muskets behind him and McAllister was the worst kind of criminal. Even if he hadn't attacked the colonial's transport, McAllister would have found some reason to lock him away in the Tolbooth.

Farr lay on the ground where he had fallen. There was blood seeping through the arm of his uniform. The pathetic boy looked as if he were about to cry.

'His arm needs setting,' the prisoner said.

It was a challenge.

'Don't concern yourself about the welfare of my men,' McAllister advised. 'I know what's best for them. On your feet, Farr.'

The boy didn't move.

'On your *feet!*' McAllister repeated sharply.

With a groan, the boy slowly pulled himself to his feet. The prisoner made to help him, but a nod from McAllister made sure that three muskets pushed him back again. All he could do was glare impotently as Farr tried to straighten himself into attention, whilst still holding his arm. It looked like it was broken: he would be no use for the moment.

'Sir,' Farr said weakly.

'Get yourself to the infirmary,' McAllister ordered.

'Sir,' Farr repeated.

He stood for a moment, swaying, and looked back up the hill he had tumbled down. McAllister said nothing. He turned to the prisoner, who looked as if he might have some words for the occasion but was biting them back. So he was clever enough to know that McAllister wouldn't take any suggestions in front of his men.

'You two,' McAllister barked at the two muskets furthest back. 'Help him get there.'

The prisoner didn't say anything. But his eyes said thank you. McAllister kept his face blank, and paced over to the prisoner, standing behind him to face his men. Eight muskets stared back at him, and he knew if he'd done his job right, at least three of the soldiers holding them would be tempted to fire: there wasn't a leader alive who could be loved *and* effective. The prisoner didn't turn though; he had military blood in him somewhere, and resisted the urge to face the enemy.

'My men tell me you have a passable Scots accent,' McAllister said casually.

'Well,' the prisoner demurred.

'But I don't believe you are Scots born,' the Captain continued. He leant in close to the prisoner's ear and hissed: 'Am I right?'

'You could definitely say that,' the prisoner agreed.

'And you attacked Mr Franklin's stagecoach.' McAllister pretended to consider. 'Or did you?'

The prisoner turned and faced McAllister at last. There was something about his eyes. Not just the depth of sadness in them, or the certain fact that they had witnessed battle. No, it was simply that they didn't once flicker, didn't once try to look at anything but the Captain's face. There were ten men with muskets and, although he could no longer see them, the prisoner cared not a jot for them.

'I didn't attack that coach,' the prisoner said.

Captain McAllister nodded briskly.

'Mooney,' he called to one of the older soldiers. 'Have the prisoner taken up to the Castle and hanged.'

'Sir,' Mooney snapped and shouldered his musket.

McAllister sniffed dismissively.

'You are a Scot sympathiser,' McAllister sneered.

'Well,' the prisoner answered him with feigned disregard, 'I did know a man who fought at Culloden.'

'You may think you have a common cause with the colonials,' McAllister said, staring hard at the prisoner. 'You may even think you may learn from each other. But let me tell you: for fifty years England and Scotland have faced their fortunes together, and together they shall face them for a hundred more. Whatever your unpatriotic kind may do. Take him away.'

Mooney stepped forward to obey his orders.

'There is just one thing,' the prisoner said casually.

Now it would come, McAllister thought. The depressingly familiar protestations of innocence, followed inevitably by the cries of justification and the outrage at the English subjugation of the noble Scot. McAllister had served here for ten years, and he knew there was nothing noble about them: the more he endured, the more he thanked the Lord that his parents had seen fit to escape to London and raise him properly there.

'The Loch,' the prisoner said instead. 'I bet it's had quite a few ghost sightings in its time, yes?'

McAllister raised an eyebrow. 'The stagnant water gives rise to vapours that gather in the Closes and make the weak-minded think they have seen things. Only a fool would believe anything otherwise.'

'Oh, of course,' the prisoner said, nodding in agreement. Why hadn't Mooney taken him yet? What was the man staring at? 'Except of course, we're not in the Closes now, and I don't think they look like scotch mist.'

McAllister's men were all staring over his shoulder, their mouths hanging slack in a manner that shamed their uniforms. The prisoner didn't seem so surprised, so clearly whatever trick this was he'd been well warned of it. He nodded over McAllister's shoulder, an expression of innocence on his face intended to convince his captor that he wouldn't bolt.

All the same, McAllister looked.

His mouth fell open.

The thick, dank waters of the Nor' Loch were just a few feet away from where they stood, and they boiled in a way that was not natural. Stinking gas broke from every bubble, filling the air with a thick sulphurous mist. McAllister couldn't tell if it was simply the product of the boiling of the waste the townsfolk had been dumping in the water for years. Somehow, it didn't seem important to ask.

Coming up out of the water were dozens of weed-strewn corpses.

Each was walking.

SIX

As the cart jostled and jiggled through the streets, Martha gradually slid herself from under her pale travelling companion. She even made it to the edge of the cart and lifted the tarpaulin. She couldn't see anything of the street except for the cobbles below rolling by, but at least it let some fresh air and a thin trickle of light into the cart. As her eyes adjusted, Martha could see the body reasonably well.

She knew what the Doctor would do.

Part of her really wanted to do what her brother Leo would do, which was to close his eyes, pretend that none of this was happening and jump out of the cart at the earliest opportunity. But she hadn't joined the Doctor on his travels because she wanted new scenery to be a coward in and, besides everything else, she was a doctor. Nearly. Since the Doctor couldn't seem to make up his mind between being 'not that sort of doctor' and 'a doctor of nearly everything', he might need a proper professional diagnosis of their zombie.

Martha folded the tarpaulin back a little to let more light in, and wished very hard that she hadn't called the body a zombie. If she just thought of it as a body – just a normal, everyday body like the kind they used in anatomy classes – then she wouldn't have to think of it suddenly coming alive and trying to eat her brains.

The skin was cool and clammy, like damp marble in the early morning, and it was pretty certain that the body had been dead for a day or two. The autopsy scar ran down his chest, red and vivid and bound together with black surgical thread. Martha opened the body's shirt a little further to see how far it went down, and then found herself looking at the chest instead: the body had been shot through the heart. There was no blood, on his clothes or in the wound itself. Martha could only assume that it had happened post-mortem, when the body was attacking the stagecoach on the Cowgate.

Perhaps, Martha thought, it was the bullet that had killed him for the second time: perhaps whatever they were dealing with here needed the heart to keep the zombies going.

She looked carefully at the bullet wound, having

to almost press her nose against it to see in the dim light. There were little hairs growing out of the edges, all arranged in a neat line around the heart. No, not hairs... more surgical thread. Whoever had performed the autopsy had sewn something onto the body's chest. Was it just coincidence that this particular body had been up and running around again? Was it coincidence that, now whatever had been sewn on was gone, the body had stopped?

Was it coincidence that when the sun went down it got dark?

She had to let the Doctor know: there might be something that the body could still tell him, but somewhere out there on the Cowgate was whatever had been shot off the zombie's chest. They had to find it before someone else found it and took it away... especially if that someone was whoever had sewn it on in the first place.

It took Martha a few moments to realise that it had suddenly gotten a lot lighter. She looked behind her, and saw a red-coated soldier with a tarpaulin in his hand and a surprised expression on his face.

Martha smiled up at him. 'It's all right,' she said. 'I'm a doctor.'

She heard a snort of disbelief at that. Looking around, she saw that the cart had come to a stop in a large courtyard surrounded by large stone buildings.

Standing outside the nearest were two men dressed in long dark robes, one a good thirty years older than the other. The older man had thick black eyebrows and a rather large nose, with a face that seemed to have been extended downwards simply because his neck wouldn't have made it up that far. The younger looked almost exactly the same, only – well, younger. They had to be father and son.

'Do you know this girl?' the younger man asked the soldier.

The soldier looked apologetic. 'I'm sorry, Mr Monro,' he mumbled. 'There was... Something happened on the Cowgate today. She was involved.'

'He was involved,' Martha protested, pointing to the corpse. 'Somebody sewed something to him and it made him get up and walk about. I know it sounds crazy, but it's true: you can see the thread on his chest. Look.'

The soldier didn't look.

'You say she was involved?' the older man said nervously. 'How so?'

'A stagecoach driver lost control of his horses,' the soldier said. Martha could tell he was choosing his words carefully; she suspected that he had seen the pale body in the cart standing on top of the stagecoach as clearly as she had. 'She stepped out in front of them.'

'Oh dear, oh dear!' exclaimed the older man.

'Excuse me?' Martha said.

She was ignored.

'I'm sorry that she has put you through so much trouble,' the younger man, Mr Monro, said to the soldier. 'She is, as you can tell, quite troubled. We should have done more to find her when we realised she was missing, shouldn't we father?'

The older man merely blinked at his son.

'You know the girl, Mr Monro?' the soldier asked.

'Oh, I—' stammered the older man.

His son jumped to his aid. 'She was placed in our care some months ago. She is an orphan, and suffers from strange fantasies. But she helps us as best she can, doing chores. Cleaning, and the like.'

Martha bristled at that. 'I'm a doctor!' she protested.

'Of course, my dear,' Monro said, slickly patronising her.

Martha sighed and held up her hand. 'Distal,' she said, pointing with her other hand.

She didn't get any further. Monro put an arm around her in a fatherly gesture of comfort, and pulled her sharply to the doorway. His arm seemed to be made of steel, it gripped her so tightly. Much as she was against the idea, it looked like she was going inside.

'Come now, let's get you to your room,' he said firmly.

'Mr Monro,' the soldier said.

Both men turned back to him.

'Yes,' they said as one.

The soldier looked flustered.

'Forgive me,' he said. 'I meant the junior.'

'Please, don't trouble yourself,' the son said with a smile, still pushing Martha towards the door. 'You can tell your captain that if he needs her, young… Mary will be here.'

'My name's Martha!' Martha protested to the soldier.

'Quiet, Mary,' the young Monro ordered. 'You may leave the body there: I shall ask one of the orderlies to collect it. We were most embarrassed about having mislaid it. Mr King may have been a vagabond in life, but in death he shall be invaluable to our students.'

The Doctor had been right: Martha didn't know as much as she should about the history of medicine. She'd been assuming that things worked pretty much the same as they did in her time, where surgeons were the people who operated on the sick and made them better.

She'd forgotten for a while how different things were in the eighteenth century, that surgeons had a whole raft of other jobs that by her time were done by different specialists. She'd forgotten that they were teachers too.

She'd forgotten that they carried out autopsies.

As the younger Monro pulled Martha over the threshold of the Surgeon's Hall, she briefly considered crying out one last time for the soldier's help. He seemed nervous enough about leaving Martha with the two surgeons – probably afraid of what Captain McAllister would do when he heard that one of his escaped prisoners had been left in the care of two civilians – and might be persuaded to rescue her if she made it clear that Monro was lying.

She didn't cry out.

The soldier wanted to take her to prison and have her securely locked up while they continued the hunt for the Doctor. If she went with him, she'd just have to wait for the Doctor to rescue her. If she stayed here, with the men who had done whatever had been done to the corpse to make it walk again, she might learn something useful. There was no real contest.

She kept quiet, and listened to the Monros bicker.

'Why did you do that?' the father asked nervously.

The younger man snorted. 'She saw King walking,' he said, pushing Martha in front of him. The corridor was long and without doors: with them behind her, she could only go forward. 'There would have been questions.'

'And what are we going to do with her?'

'I don't know.'

'Alexander!'

'Be quiet!' the younger man snapped, and surprisingly his father obeyed. 'We are nearly finished here. It worked: you heard what she said about King. There is no reason to delay any longer. We keep her here for the next few hours, and then what does it matter? Everyone will know. Stop fussing. Is the theatre prepared?'

'You know it is,' the father answered sulkily.

'Well then.'

'Excuse me,' Martha said, stopping and turning.

The two men looked at her.

'Aren't you even going to ask who I am?'

'You are an annoyance,' the younger Monro said.

'Oh I'm more than that,' Martha said. She planted her hands on her hips and gave a defiant stare. 'I know what you're up to: bringing people back from the dead. That's pretty freaky stuff. What are you? Aliens? Witches? Alien witches?'

The two men just looked at her blankly.

'We're the Chair of Anatomy,' the older Monro said, more than a little confused.

'The Chair of Anatomy?' Martha echoed. 'Is that your species?'

'It's our position,' he answered. 'In the University.'

Martha felt her cheeks flush.

'Right,' she said, trying to keep the upper hand. 'But I bet your university doesn't know what you're up to here, does it?'

'And exactly what are we up to?' the young Monro asked icily.

They did have her there.

'Sewing things to dead bodies?' she tried. 'Look, why don't you just tell me everything before you get into any more trouble? It'd look better for you at the trial.'

'Trial?' the older Monro echoed nervously.

His son ignored him. 'Mary,' he said.

'*Martha*,' she corrected.

'Would you like to know what we attached to the vagabond King's chest?' Alexander Monro asked.

Martha gave the anatomist a cautious look. 'OK,' she said slowly.

Alexander Monro smiled and turned to the wall beside him. He pressed his palms against it, and a section of the wall pressed inwards, before swinging back out to reveal a doorway. Martha looked carefully through the hidden door, but the room inside was in complete darkness, except for some greasy light fighting through a smudged and dirty window in the far wall. She thought she heard the sound of something scuttling inside.

She looked at the younger Monro.

He smiled back, and pushed her in.

The junior Mr Monro slid the door quickly shut, and within seconds it was as if it had never existed. He couldn't even hear the sounds of the girl – *Martha* – shouting on the other side. The craftsmen he had paid had been well worth the money and the effort. Now he could concentrate on other things.

'You should not have done that,' the senior Monro admonished.

But the younger just walked away, without a second glance.

Martha turned and pressed her back against the door, letting out a sigh. She slid slowly to the floor and spent a second resting her chin on her knees. She wondered briefly if it was time to have another of those goodbye arguments with her mother.

Something moved in the far corner.

Martha peered through the gloom, but the window was barely the size of her two fists and was covered in dust and cobwebs. She pulled herself back up to her feet and told herself she should take a step forward. She didn't, though.

'Hello?' she said cautiously. 'My name's Martha.'

She heard another sound, coming from a different

direction. It sounded uncomfortably like something scuttling across a stone floor. She really wished she'd paid more attention in history classes. Did they have tarantulas in eighteenth-century Scotland?

Her hands started brushing up and down the walls as she tried to find the hidden switch that would open the door. Instead, they came across something cold and metal attached to the wall. Feeling it up and down, she found it was a little saucer filled with something slick and wet, with a small piece of string poking out of it. Martha realised that it was a lamp, and that she had dipped her fingers into whatever the fuel was: a quick sniff told her it was fish oil. She gritted her teeth.

She put her hands in her pockets and rummaged around as quietly as she could. All the time, the sounds of scuttling were starting to grow: the light as the door had opened had probably startled whatever was in here, but now they were starting to wake up. There was definitely more than one of the things in here: she could hear them scurrying from all sides of the room now. Her heart jumped as she heard a dry click near to her feet and suddenly thought that her roommates might be crabs. Crabs brought back decidedly mixed emotions.

Her hand found what it was looking for in her left pocket: a small box of matches with a gaudy Grampus scrawled across them. They were a souvenir of a brief stop-off at a bar on Io that the Doctor had insisted she see: everyone who worked in the place was a dolphin, walking around with the aid of sleek mechanical legs and talking with a calm, Stephen Hawking-style electronic voice. Even the dancers.

Martha lit a match, then the lamp.

Then turned.

The lamp seemed to give off more smoke than light, but Martha's eyes quickly adjusted. She could see most of the room, in a sort of misty early morning kind of a way: stone floors, stone walls and a wooden chair and table at the far end with a metal plate resting on it. Every available bit of space at the far end of the room was filled with them. They were on the chair, on the table, clinging to the walls and trying to reach the dirty little window. Except now they were all frozen, sensing the light on them, despite the fact that they didn't have any eyes that Martha could see.

She thought that she was right, and that they were crabs.

Then she saw that she was wrong.

The hands quivered slightly, standing on four fingers whilst the index stood high, the neck to a fingernail head. Each had a wrist at their back end, rising up to a rounded stump of smooth grey flesh. These hands hadn't been cut off, but gave the impression of having been born like this, discrete little units. One of them stood at Martha's feet, its back to her. Martha shuffled her feet slightly to get away from it, but she was already pressed tight against the door. Part of her was already thinking that these must have been what Alexander Monro had sewn to the body.

Gradually, each of the twitching hands began to turn, the animal instinct sweeping across them like a wave. The index fingers didn't seem to have eyes, ears or mouths, but somehow Martha could feel every one of them looking at her. There must be a hundred or more of them, all locked in this tiny little room with her. She wondered whether shouting would make anybody come. And, if anyone did, would they be able to find the hidden door?

There was more scuttling, and suddenly each of the hands was hurrying across the floor towards her. The one at her feet gave a little flex of its fingers and jumped onto her foot, scurrying fast up her legs. Martha gave a little cry and kicked out: the hand flew across the room and landed in the middle of a knot of its fellows. It picked itself up with a little shake and hurried back towards her.

They were all around her, climbing up the cracks in the stone work to get closer to her face, or cautiously tapping at her feet as they tried to decide whether the climb was worth it. More and more of them seemed to be appearing from nowhere, and it was clear that in a matter of seconds Martha would be completely smothered by them. She tried to think, but she couldn't help seeing them as little spiders that were going to crawl all over her and... she didn't want to think what they would do once there wasn't an inch of Martha left visible any more.

A hand landed on her shoulder, and before she could shake it off two more jumped from the wall and landed in her hair. The hands around her feet began to move onto her shoes, and caress her ankles. Martha closed her eyes tight and tried to think something useful.

The light.

Before she'd turned the light on, they'd been happy enough jumping up at the window. Perhaps they were just crawling up her to get at the light: if she blew it out, they might go back to climbing the walls at the other side of the room. It seemed like a good idea: the only downside was that it would leave her standing in near pitch darkness, with strange little hands crawling all over her like insects.

Maybe her mother was right: she shouldn't be travelling with the Doctor. How did she get herself into trouble like this?

She leant over and blew out the lamp.

Everything went black.

SEVEN

There was a strange moment of silence. All the soldiers, even Captain McAllister, stood immobile and watched as the figures rose out of the water.

They looked so much like people – wet, weed-strewn, pale-skinned people – and yet they walked so slowly that their heads were held deep under the water for much longer than any human could hold their breath. There was no gasping for air as their heads broke the surface, just the dribble of the filthy waters running from their mouths and noses.

Their eyes were open as they walked, blind white and staring glassily ahead. Their arms hung limply by their sides.

'What are they?' McAllister breathed.

The Doctor saw the creatures' clothes still clinging

to them, damp and rotten with the water: the style of dress varied from fifteenth-century farmer's wives through to soldiers who might only have fallen into the water the day before. Each was as remarkably well preserved as the next, despite their varying ages. Was there something in the water that was preserving them?

'People,' the Doctor answered. 'Or they were…'

'It's witchcraft,' one of the younger soldiers cried, and dropped his musket.

Before it even touched the ground, McAllister spun.

'Attention!' he barked in his best parade-ground voice.

The Doctor watched the creatures in the water that were dressed as soldiers. If there was anything human left in them, they might respond to something as ingrained as military training. They just kept moving blankly onwards.

McAllister tried again. 'You men will come to order!'

For just a fraction of a second, it looked like the soldiers would lose their nerve. Then each of them made the decision that they were more afraid of Captain McAllister than they were of the walking dead and snapped to attention. The soldier who had dropped his musket bent hurriedly and scooped it up;

when he stood, he was holding it upside down over his shoulder and had to quickly spin it.

'The city is under attack,' McAllister said.

'They don't seem to be attacking,' the Doctor corrected.

'Our duty is to defend it to the last man,' McAllister continued regardless. 'Form two defensive lines, and fire on my command.'

The soldiers quickly dropped back into two lines, the first kneeling on the ground and shouldering their muskets, whilst the second stood behind them and waited. The Doctor looked down at the bodies as they walked out of the stinking Loch: they weren't co-ordinated, and they weren't attacking. They didn't look like they had any goal in mind other than getting out of the mire – which, admittedly, was rather more ambition than humans were comfortable with from their corpses, but didn't necessarily indicate an invasion.

'Wait.' The Doctor spoke quietly to McAllister. If the Captain's men overheard, then he would automatically do the opposite of whatever the Doctor requested just to save face. 'I don't think they're attacking. We should wait and see what they do: they might be friendly.'

'Indeed,' McAllister agreed curtly. 'I'm certain they wish to thank us for leaving them to rot in the city's filth.'

The Doctor looked again at the blank-eyed corpses.

They were nearly out of the water.

'They haven't seen us,' he insisted.

But McAllister had turned away.

'Fire!' he bellowed.

The five soldiers kneeling on the ground fired as one, their muskets belching smoke into the air. The moment the triggers were pulled, the five men behind them took two paces forward and knelt, bringing their muskets up. Behind them, the first five stood and quickly reloaded their weapons. It was a marvellously efficient system, allowing an almost constant barrage of fire even with the muskets' lengthy reload time.

It was going to get them all killed, of course.

'Fire!' McAllister yelled again.

The kneeling soldiers fired, and the lines rotated again, moving closer to their targets with each shot.

The musketballs found their targets easily, since the walking dead were making no effort to shield themselves. Of the first five shots, three found their targets. Of the next five, none missed. One corpse was struck in the shoulder, tearing the smock he had on and sending a small shower of dust into the air. It didn't even stop. Another was struck in the stomach: a small hole punched straight through its middle and made it stagger back into the water for a single step.

Then it looked about with its blind eyes, and seemed to see the soldiers. The Doctor felt a sudden chill as those perfectly white eyes fell momentarily on him. There was a strange feeling of intelligence there, and almost surprise that it was being attacked.

'Stop!' the Doctor shouted.

The creature's eyes fell on the soldiers as another round of musketballs were fired. Its mouth fell open and it let out an inhuman hiss, like an enraged cat. All around it, the other corpses all stopped and turned. As one, their mouths opened and they too hissed. The air all around was filled with the sound of their anger, and even McAllister had cause to pause.

'Fire!' he shouted again, and the moment broke.

Even before the soldiers could obey the order, each of the creatures turned to face them and started to run. Their outstretched arms each had a set of fingernails that seemed to be carved of steel and which glinted in the sunlight. There was no doubt that they could tear out a throat in a single swipe.

'Fire!' McAllister ordered again.

Smoke filled the air, but not a single one of the bodies fell to the ground. It would take just a few more seconds, and they would be on top of the soldiers.

'Retreat!' came the order.

The soldiers didn't even look about to see where it had come from. As one, they abandoned the line and turned and fled. McAllister looked around for a moment, and when his eyes fell on the Doctor they were almost black with anger. The Doctor just glared back coldly. For a moment, there was no one there but the two of them, and the Doctor knew that, if McAllister ever had the chance, he would kill him. The Captain would have to join the back of a very long queue for that one, and only then if the Doctor managed to get him out of this alive.

But just for the moment, McAllister could either pretend he had given the order, or admit that he'd lost control of his men. McAllister turned and hurried after the soldiers.

'Keep together,' he barked as he ran. 'You're soldiers, not fishwives.'

The creatures kept coming out of the Loch, and each one that did was already bearing down on the soldiers. There were perhaps two hundred of them now, emerging from the water and pacing up the hill without pause. The soldiers hurried away in front of them, but even for trained men it was a difficult climb to run. They puffed and they panted and they stumbled as they ran. The creatures didn't slow, didn't tire, and didn't even seem to breathe. As the Doctor ran behind, he noticed something else far more troubling.

'Captain McAllister,' he shouted.

McAllister didn't stop, didn't turn.

'They're going to beat us to the top,' the Doctor yelled.

That gave the Captain pause for just a moment as he hurriedly glanced up the line of his men. It was obviously true: in fact, some of the creatures had started to swing to the right and would intercept the hurrying soldiers before they were even halfway up. McAllister froze, almost imperceptibly. His eyes widened as he tried to come up with the perfect tactic for escape, and failed. The Doctor was by his side instantly.

'We have to go down,' he said.

'Are you mad?'

'Look at them,' the Doctor insisted. 'Most of the creatures are moving up to block the route to the Castle: if we go down, we might have a chance.'

'If we don't run straight into a den of smugglers,' the Captain argued. 'If they see a troop of soldiers running for them, do think they'll wait to ask what we're doing before they open fire?

'Smugglers have boats,' the Doctor hissed.

McAllister looked into the Doctor's eyes, and nodded.

'This way, men!' he ordered.

The soldiers turned, but none of them stopped running. The creatures were closing in all around, and all they could think of was the possibility of getting back behind strong castle walls. Even if none of them would ever make it.

'I said follow me!' McAllister barked angrily. 'Or I'll shoot every last one of you myself!'

If it was an act, it was a convincing one. McAllister glanced at the Doctor, and then led the charge back down the hill. As one, his men charged behind him, all heading for the shore where the Loch bent around the foot of the hill.

The Doctor took a moment to watch the creatures as they were wrong-footed: some slid a little on the grass as they suddenly tried to turn and switch directions, but some were already above the knot of soldiers and just continued in their relentless march downwards.

'Move, man,' said the first soldier as he passed.

There was a soldier at the end of the group, a young man with short dark hair and blue eyes. He'd been at the head of the charge away, so he was the closest to the creatures that were cutting across to intercept. He was almost close enough to reach out and touch their dripping clothes. He had heard the order to turn, and might even know that it was the right thing to do, but his eyes were blind with panic. He kept on running up, trying to swing around a knot of creatures in mouldy sackcloth.

'No!' the Doctor shouted, pacing forwards. 'This way.'

It was too late. It had already been too late when the Doctor had first spotted him. The knot of creatures reached out with pale, slimy hands and, although the soldier managed to pull away from some, more of the hands held tight. He was pulled down into the middle of the creatures with a loud scream, and disappeared amongst them.

A few seconds later, the Doctor saw him again. His blue eyes were dead and cold, and he was marching down after his fellow soldiers with the same relentless step as the other walking dead. There was no saving him now. There might be no saving any of them.

'Come on,' urged the last soldier as he rushed by.

Reluctantly, the Doctor followed.

McAllister harried his men down to the shore of the Loch, where the ground grew damper and muddier and the marsh gas hung on the foul water. The Loch circled the rear of the Castle, cut at either end by a road leading into the city: their best hope was to circle behind the Castle and back up the Grassmarket. With any luck, they would be able to attract the attention of a few muskets on duty as they ran, and these watery devils would soon be dispatched.

His men, however, had other ideas: they had

stopped by the Loch's edge and were fretting to each other.

'Sir!' one yelled as soon as McAllister was near. 'Look!'

McAllister looked: the prisoner had been wrong. Loping towards them from the other direction were ten more of the undead creatures. McAllister and his men had no escape route now, just the decision between two groups of creatures and the dank waters of the Loch.

'This way,' the prisoner shouted, charging in behind McAllister.

The Captain expected him to stop and despair when he saw the second group of pale figures moving in on them, but he didn't. He just kept charging on – not towards them, not around the edge of the Castle, but towards the Loch and a small clump of sickly looking trees that grew there. He disappeared into them for a moment, making McAllister suddenly afraid that his only plan was to hide and hope the creatures would pass.

The trees shook, and something slid into view.

'Give me a hand, then,' the prisoner shouted.

He re-emerged, pushing a raft out of the trees and towards the Loch. McAllister's men didn't even wait for the order; they were by his side and pushing the unseaworthy vessel out into the dark waters as one.

There was just enough room for all of them to perch on it, as long as they didn't move too much, but there were no paddles to be seen: it was a smugglers' vessel, hidden there after bringing in untaxed alcohol to wait for the return journey after the goods had been sold.

Another charge to bring against the prisoner.

'Well come on then,' the man said impatiently.

McAllister stepped onto the raft, and stood proudly in the centre as his men each knelt at the sides and began frantically paddling. The raft made good speed, but McAllister could see the creatures as they reached the water's edge. They didn't pause, just walked back into it as easily as they had stepped out from it. They seemed to move with the same relentless speed.

'We have not escaped yet,' he realised.

One of McAllister's men let out a cry and snatched his hand out of the water. A pale hand broke the surface, reaching out to try to grab him. Another appeared on the port side of the raft, and then another.

'Keep paddling,' the prisoner ordered.

The waters bubbled all around them.

The Doctor knelt at the stern of the raft and alternated between steering and batting away searching hands with the only paddle he'd been able to find on the boat. There were still several creatures under the water, but they seemed to be having difficulty floating up to reach the raft – probably understandable considering how long most of them must have been down there. The ones who were following them from the other side also sank quickly below the surface and gave chase at the same measured pace as they had on land.

Except for the soldier. Their most recent victim.

'What was his name?' the Doctor asked McAllister.

'Who?'

The Doctor pointed behind them. The soldier seemed to be swimming after them, but a strange stroke somewhere between floating and walking. In truth, he was more buoyant than his companions, and would have found it difficult to walk along the bottom as they did.

McAllister glanced quickly and turned away again. 'Wright,' he muttered. 'Ernest Wright.'

'I'm sorry,' said the Doctor, though no one alive could hear.

'There! Look!' came a panicked shout. 'They're ahead of us.'

The Doctor stood immediately. If the creatures had reached the other side before the raft, then there was little hope left. Perhaps he could modify the sonic screwdriver to ignite the pockets of marsh gas floating above the water, but that would only give them a few moments of distraction. He peered across the Loch. The soldiers had stopped paddling. There was indeed a dark figure looming on the other shore, and not all that far away.

'No,' the Doctor announced. 'That's a person.'

There was a moment's silence.

'What are you waiting for?' McAllister barked. 'Keep paddling!'

The raft jolted forward again, but the Doctor remained where he was. They were only seconds from the shore now, and there was little need to steer. Behind them, the water bubbled and churned, marking the steady submarine progress of the creatures following. It would be close. The Doctor had lost one man, he wasn't going to lose any more.

'Quickly,' the figure on the shore called. 'Quickly!'

He was a tall man, with a bald scalp pushing up through a ring of greying hair and a beard that circled the bottom of his face as if to compensate. He ran into the Loch, regardless of the water that rose up to his knees, and reached out to grab the Doctor's hands, pulling him and the raft into dock. He needn't have bothered: as soon as the raft was within wading distance of the shore, the soldiers started to leap off. By the time the Doctor jumped onto the damp grass, the soldiers were already looking around like nervous rabbits being pursued by a fox.

'This way,' the stranger said, waving them up the shore. 'Follow me.'

'To where?' McAllister asked sharply.

The stranger pointed further up the shore: there was a path that wound through some trees, and the familiar spired shape of a church waiting at the end of it. The church had two large wooden doors that looked like they could keep out the assembled hordes of Genghis Khan. McAllister nodded at the stranger, as if noticing for the first time that he was dressed in a minister's drab dark robes.

'Sir?' one of the soldiers asked.

McAllister glanced behind him, as did the Doctor. The creatures were rising again from the Loch, the water pouring from them like rain. Long green weeds clung to their ancient clothes. Somewhere on his journey, Ernest Wright had torn his bright red jacket.

'Follow the minister,' McAllister ordered.

He didn't have to say it twice.

It was a short run along the path and up to the church, but none of the soldiers said a word as they ran. The Doctor suspected that each of them was thinking the same thing: between the path and the church doors, the graveyard sat. So far, the only creatures they had seen had all risen from the Loch, but that didn't mean that it would stay that way. All it would take was for one creature to appear from behind the shadows of a grave, and that would be that.

The graveyard was filled with trees as well as headstones, and there were plenty of shadows to choose between. The graves themselves were mostly decorated with carefully carved skulls laughing out at the living. The Doctor imagined that more than one of the soldiers wished that the city's masons had had a less literal frame of mind.

They hurried through the maze of stones, the minister shouting encouragement from the Doctor's side. The creatures were only yards behind them.

'Inside,' the minister called. 'There are others waiting. Don't worry.'

The Doctor, McAllister and the minister were the last to enter the church, and the frontrunners of their pale pursuers almost had their fingers in the doors. It took all three of them to slam shut the doors behind them and draw the heavy bolts across. For a moment, nobody said anything. The minister and McAllister just stood and panted. Behind them, the church was silent.

'Don't worry,' the minister said in hushed tones. 'St Cuthbert's kept our congregation safe when it was the Pretender at the doors. She'll keep us safe now.'

The Doctor opened his mouth to say something.

But he was drowned out by the sound of hammering on the doors.

The creatures had arrived.

EIGHT

Martha stood blind in the sudden darkness, her back pressed tight against the hidden door. She could hear the disembodied hands scuttling all around her. She told herself calmly that they were probably moving back to the murky light from the window, and not to panic. Her heart pounded roughly in her chest. She blinked hard and often, trying to get her eyes used to the darkness again. All she could see was the flicker of the oil lamp that was no longer lit.

Something brushed against her arm, and she let out a yelp and jumped to one side. She banged her elbow against the wall as she moved, and a tingling numbness shot down to her fingers.

'Stop it,' she told herself sharply. 'Just… stop it.' She closed her eyes for a moment, and breathed deeply.

When she opened them again, her eyes had grown more accustomed to the darkness. She could see the strange grey hands had lost interest in her and were indeed scuttling back to worship at the greasy window. She could see them as little pale shapes, thronging here and there, trying to climb the wall to reach the light just as they'd tried to climb her. So she was right: they were attracted to the light.

But there seemed to be more to it than that. The way they moved, slumping as if tired but frantically scrabbling to climb the cold walls; the way that some of them fell from the walls and lay on their sides for a few moments, as if they were trying to decide whether it was actually worth getting up again. As she watched, Martha realised that she wasn't the only one being kept in the room against her will.

'Erm, hello?' she said, taking a step forward.

She felt more than a little stupid: what kind of response exactly was she expecting when the hands didn't seem to have ears, eyes or mouths? But the Doctor would have tried to communicate with them. As a doctor, so should she.

'Can you understand me?' she asked in a clearer voice.

A small knot of hands on the floor seemed to turn and look at her. She knelt and looked at them, stopping short of holding out her hand to theirs. They each had a wart growing at the base of their index fingers... the base of their necks, she imagined. The fingers were criss-crossed at the tips with a multitude of tiny white scars where the skin had been nicked and healed a thousand times over the years. The pattern of the scars was identical from one hand to the next. They were all the same hand.

'Can you . . ?' she stopped herself. If they couldn't understand her, there was no point in asking. 'I don't know what you are: I've never seen anything like this before. But I've got this friend, the Doctor. He'll know what's going on. He'll lend... he'll be able to help you, I mean.'

Martha felt her cheeks flush a little.

The hands turned away and redoubled their efforts to try and reach the tiny window in the corner.

Martha knew that she could reach it if she went over there. Perhaps she could clean it with her sleeve and see whatever it was that it overlooked. Perhaps a whole platoon of soldiers who'd be quick to break the door down and rescue her. More likely a gang of drunken medical students laughing at their old teachers who hadn't even heard of the miraculous properties of leeches.

If she let the hands crawl up her body, they might even be able to break the glass themselves. Then at least they could escape and perhaps, like Androcles' lion, they'd find some way to help her in the future. But somehow she couldn't quite bring herself to do it. Something about the way those fingers scurried and danced, something about how closely they resembled overgrown spiders.

Instead, she stood by the wall and tried to think of something clever.

Martha didn't know how long she stood there, but it felt like it might have been days. The hands in the corner of the room still scampered and climbed, but none of them had yet managed to get within jumping distance of the window. She'd noticed that they seemed to be taking it in turns, one group trying whilst another huddled together in the darkness and seemed to sleep. Still she didn't step over to help them.

The tapping came quietly, from the wall behind her.

The hands didn't react.

'Hello?' she said.

'Step away from the door,' came a muffled voice.

Martha's heart skipped at the thought that it might be the Doctor, somehow come to save her, but his voice she would have known even through the vaults of the Bank of England. No, this must be one of the two Mr Monros, come to do whatever it was they'd had in mind when they locked her in here in the first place.

She couldn't tell if it was the older or the younger. She wondered if it really made a difference.

She stepped away from the door.

It slid open silently, and for a moment the light blinded her. The hands suddenly scurried for the opening, a mass of fingers and thumbs all dancing over the stone floor.

Then the light was gone. Martha didn't think any of the little creatures had escaped. She had an afterimage of Mr Monro the elder standing in the room, carrying a clay jar with two metal prongs coming from it and wearing an apologetic look, but then the darkness took it.

'I am sorry,' Monro said. 'Please believe me, we mean you no harm.'

'Really?' Martha said. If her sarcasm had been water, it would have filled the hidden room and drowned them both. 'You locked us in here for our own good, did you?'

Monro at least had the decency to be embarrassed. 'The goal we are working towards…' He stopped. 'You are right, of course. It is inexcusable. You may go free at once. Alexander is away collecting… He will not know that you are gone, I promise. I will not ask you to keep what has happened to you here a secret. If you choose to return with the bailies, that will be your decision.'

'Bailies?' Martha asked. As far as she was concerned, Baileys was a drink you had with ice or coffee.

Martha's eyes were adjusting to the darkness again: she could just make out Monro looking at her with understanding.

'You are from London,' he said, as if sorry for her. 'They call the magistrates bailies hereabouts. By the time you return, we will have completed our work, I hope. But if we have not, perhaps that is as well.'

'And what exactly is your work?' Martha asked.

Monro gave her a look.

'You should leave without delay,' he said. 'Alexander will not be long.'

Martha took a step back and folded her arms firmly across her chest. She didn't much want to spend the rest of her life trapped in this dark room with a load of disembodied hands, but if Monro was saying that whatever he and his son had planned would be done by the time she got back with the Doctor... She'd seen enough old horror movies to know that mad scientists were very rarely working to reduce global warming or feed the starving masses of the world.

'I am sorry,' he said softly. 'But I cannot delay for you.'

Martha didn't move.

Monro shrugged and stepped forward, setting his clay pot on the ground and looking around him for a moment. It was clear that he was looking for the hands, but with the door shut they had gone back to trying to climb for the window. He nodded to himself, as if this was only to be expected, and reached down to pull at the pot's two prongs: they came away, revealing themselves to be the ends of two dirty copper wires. It was only then that Martha realised that Monro was wearing thick leather gloves.

Copper wires and protective clothing. Martha realised that the clay pot was some sort of eighteenth-century battery. She was going to question whether they even had electricity that long ago, but then she remembered the stagecoach's passenger: Benjamin Franklin, who had famously flown a kite in a thunderstorm to collect electricity from the lightning. If he was doing it, then there was no reason why Monro couldn't be as well. Perhaps the jar contained bottled lightning drawn down during some recent Edinburgh downpour.

Monro leant over a stray hand, and touched the two wires to it.

Martha let out a gasp as the hand suddenly went into a spasm, its fingers stretching out with a crack that left it lying flat on the floor. The reaction was so violent, that Martha wouldn't have been surprised if one of the fingers or more had been broken. Monro didn't flinch, just picked up the twitching hand and dropped it into a rough sack at his side. Then he repeated the process with another hand.

'Stop it!' Martha shouted.

'I assure you, there is no harm,' Monro said, turning to her as he bent to pick up the second hand. 'There is no brain to feel the pain: I have dissected them to be certain. They recover within moments, without any sign of permanent—'

Monro stopped abruptly. While he had been looking at Martha, one of the hands had taken the opportunity to creep closer to him, unnoticed. Then, suddenly, it had tensed and sprung. It bounced up to Monro as he crouched, and gripped his shirt so tightly that the fingernails were drawing tiny droplets of blood into the white fabric. The hand was holding itself tightly over Monro's heart.

Monro gave a cry of pain. Without thinking, Martha rushed forwards and grabbed the two copper wires from Monro's hands. There was a slight tingle and nothing more, so these clay batteries couldn't exactly be high power. But the reaction when she brushed the wires against the hand was dramatic: Monro gave a loud cry and fell to the floor, and the hand twitched so violently that it pushed itself off the old man's chest and across to the far side of the room.

The other hands scuttled to avoid it, forming a ring and craning their index fingers towards it. Then, almost as one, they all turned to point at Martha and Monro. Martha, crouching by the old man's side and checking his heart, suddenly felt very aware that the door was shut.

'The lintel,' Monro gasped. 'The switch.'

Martha stood, not turning her back on the hands while she ran her own over the top of the hidden door. She felt an invisible button depress, and suddenly the door swung inwards, narrowly missing Monro's bare head. Martha grabbed him by the shoulders and tugged him swiftly out of the doorway. His hand was still clutching the sack, and two disembodied hands struggled and fought inside it. The rest of them flung themselves in Martha's direction. She told herself they were just after their freedom, but it was too hard to believe that they weren't trying to reach her.

She pulled the door shut just in time.

Then she slid to the floor with her back against it, panting hard. Monro lay at her feet, his eyes open but his breathing ragged. Behind her, she could hear the sound of the hands flinging themselves against it, one after the other. It sounded like raindrops falling. She told herself that they only wanted their freedom. She told herself that if she knew how, she would have turned and opened the door to help them.

She didn't move.

***

The colour had drained from Monro's face, but he managed to pull himself upright and catch his breath. He looked so bewildered that Martha couldn't help but feel sorry for him. It also served as a prick to her conscience: instead of sitting against the door doing nothing, she knew that she should be checking the old anatomist over to see if the attacking hand had done any serious damage.

'They… it…' Monro stammered, holding a hand to his heart.

Martha leant over and gently took his arm.

'Don't worry,' she told him. 'You've had a shock, but you're safe now.'

He turned to her, surprise in his eyes. 'It learnt,' he said.

Martha didn't say anything, just began checking Monro for injuries: the hand's fingernail had dug fairly deep into the skin of his chest, but other than that it seemed just to be the shock of it. The five half-crescent punctures that surrounded his heart were already drying, looking like some kind of ill-judged tattoo.

'Don't you see?' Monro asked her, his hand gripping Martha's arm tightly. 'It learnt. It *learnt!*'

Martha gently prised her arm free. 'Learnt what?'

'The first hand,' he said. There was a catch in his voice that Martha thought might be asthma. 'I had to sew it to Arthur King's chest and even then it struggled. But now… that hand clung on itself. It learnt how to take hold of a body. It tried to… I could feel it, in my mind. Such a…'

Monro looked through Martha: she wasn't even there.

'The two hands have never been in contact,' he whispered. 'But the one learnt from the other. This is…'

Martha didn't want to speak, afraid that she might break the spell and Monro would see her again. But staying quiet wouldn't help anybody. There were questions that needed to be asked, things she needed to know. If they were going to stop whatever this was, they couldn't just sit back and say nothing.

'You sewed the hand to a dead body?' Martha asked.

'If you'd seen the miracles it had already performed…' was Monro's only answer.

'You brought that man back to life?' she pressed, leaning in close. 'And made him attack the stagecoach?'

'No no. It escaped. I have no idea why it attacked—'

There was a sound from further down the corridor, a sharp metallic scraping. Monro heard it, and suddenly his eyes cleared. Now he was looking at Martha, and he was seeing her. She looked at him, another question on her lips, but it was too late. He was already on his feet, clutching the rough sack in one hand and looking down the corridor in panic.

'Alexander has returned,' he whispered. 'You must hide. The auditorium is at the end of this corridor. You can stay there until you can escape.'

'But—'

'No, you must go,' Monro hissed sharply. 'Or—'

'Father?' came a shout from further down the corridor. 'Come help, old man.'

Monro turned to Martha. 'Go,' he said. Then he hurried down the corridor.

For much less than a moment, Martha considered ignoring his advice, considered following Monro to confront his son, like the Doctor would. She could hear the younger Monro arguing with his father further down the corridor. It sounded like they were trying to drag a wardrobe down after them, with much banging and scraping of wood across stone walls. The experience didn't seem to be making either of them any more cheerful. Perhaps it wouldn't be so bad to hide and watch the anatomists.

She hurried down the corridor until she came out in a large gaslit room filled with rows of seats looking down on a dark-stained wooden table. Beside it was another, smaller table that glistened with medical instruments, most of which Martha could name despite there being two and a half centuries between her hospital and 1759. It was a lecture hall, quite obviously. Monro or his son would stand at the table, and row after row of students would watch and take notes as the demonstration progressed.

Martha heard a noise behind her, and remembered that she wasn't alone. She hurried down to the end of a row and ducked down behind the seats. Looking back behind her, she could only see a very thin sliver of the rest of the room. She heard them before she saw them, bickering and panting and bumping something unwieldy down the central stairs to the waiting table.

'Be careful,' the young Monro said.

'Of course,' his father snapped.

They passed briefly into the thin field of Martha's vision, carrying a large wooden box between them. The father was at the front, taking the bulk of the weight, while the son steadied it from behind. They had passed by in a matter of moments, and the gaslights didn't exactly make it easy to see from one end of the room to the other. Even so, Martha thought she knew exactly what the box was, mouldy and muddy as it was. She just prayed that she was mistaken.

'There,' came Alexander's voice from the bottom of the room.

There was the sound of more panting and banging

and scraping, and then a soggy thud that must have been the box dropping heavily onto the table. After that, there was nothing for a few moments except the sound of old Mr Monro trying to get his breath back. Martha wondered whether she should risk peeking out at them.

'We must get ready,' Mr Monro said, more than a little stagily.

'Did you collect the hands?' his son asked.

'Here.'

'And the girl?'

There was a pause, and Martha wondered just how good an actor Monro was. Her heart began to pound as she imagined the old man's eyes flicking momentarily up to the auditorium.

'You should not have trapped her there,' Monro said sharply. 'The hands... they are beginning to show signs of anger.'

'Anger?'

'One attacked. They aim for the heart, Alexander.'

'Interesting. The heart?' Alexander gave another pause. 'And the girl was hurt?'

Martha didn't think he sounded particularly concerned.

'We must get ready,' Monro said again, colder than before.

'Yes, yes.'

And then there was the sound of a door closing, and nothing but the faint crackle of the gas lamps. Martha took a deep breath and counted to ten. Then she stood up, slowly.

The room was empty.

Except for the box.

Martha knew that Monro expected her to use this opportunity to escape. Perhaps even the Doctor would want her to: he might already have lost McAllister and be waiting at the door to be let in. Except that she knew him well enough now to know that his plans never quite worked out how he intended. There was always some kind of flaw, something he'd missed.

She didn't know how much time she had. If the two Monros came back and caught her... well, probably the best that she could hope was to be put back in the room with the hands. The angry hands that had learned to go for the heart. She should go, get the Doctor. Except that the box sat there, on the table, bowed with damp and with age. It still had something of its original shape, but all the same Martha wouldn't let herself believe it. Not until she'd checked.

She moved down the stairs.

As she got closer, the musty smell of mouldy wood assaulted her. The box smelt like it had been underground for a good few years: there was still damp earth clinging to it, here and there. But that didn't mean… She had to be sure, so she stepped up next to it. On the top – the lid – there was a little brass plaque, smeared with wet earth. She reached out with a hand and cleaned it off as best she could, revealing the engraving.

John Monro, it said. *(1670–1740)*.

NINE

Inside the church, there was that dry chill to the air – that brittle silence that was the fear of echoes the Doctor always felt in churches. It was the way they were built: massive cold stones held together by a sense of awe and then filled with the devout and the fearful. They collected energy these buildings – faith, history – and it warped the space within them.

'Hello,' the Doctor said quietly.

Because you never knew when you might get an answer.

McAllister and his soldiers were running around the church, looking for doors and windows that they could guard. The Captain barked the orders, and his men followed them in silence. That way, no one had to think about their friend Ernest, hammering on the closed and bolted church doors with the rest of the walking dead. McAllister's voice echoed around the church, seeming thin and insubstantial. In the pews, the congregation sat and huddled together, looking with wide eyes to their minister.

He stood beside the Doctor, watching his flock.

'Please,' the minister said, holding his hands up. 'Don't be afraid. The doors are bolted. Whatever they are outside, they are outside. We have time to find a solution, and we will use it.'

'There is no time, Reverend,' an old man growled from a centre pew. 'It's the end of the world. The Lord has judged us, and the dead are here to drag us down to Hell.'

There were some frightened murmurs at that, each member of the congregation turning to their friends and family and each deciding that yes, they might well have been judged badly. The Doctor made to step forward and appeal for calm, but the grey-haired minister was already cutting across the low mumbling.

'Is that right, Thomas?' he said sharply, his voice filling the cold church. 'And what sin have you committed that was so grave that Our Father could not forgive you for it even as you sat in His house and praised His name? What sin has Alf Smith committed, or Rebecca Parr and her son? No, even though we don't know it, there is some earthly reason for this. And that should give us hope, because it means we can find an earthly solution.'

'Quite right,' the Doctor agreed, flashing the minister a smile.

But doubting Thomas wasn't quite ready to give up.

'Perhaps it's not our sin, Reverend Yarwood,' he muttered darkly. 'But yours.'

There was a silence, and the minister floundered for a moment.

'And what sin would you have our Gordon commit, Thomas?' said a bear of a man pulling himself to his feet. 'One sip too many of the communion wine? Mistaking the ale house for his home? Or would that be the sins of some other?'

'I wasn't talking to you, Ralph,' Thomas spat, although his face made it quite clear he knew those sins intimately himself.

'It seems to me that we've more pressing matters at hand than casting the first stone,' the round-faced man continued. 'Those poor souls are outside, and we are here. Perhaps we would be best served making sure we can keep things that way?'

There was a general murmur of agreement, and the congregation automatically looked to the man to tell them what to do next. There was something in his very presence that seemed to reassure them. Before he could speak, one of the soldiers shouted from the window.

'The creatures are standing back.'

'Well,' the Doctor said with a smile. 'That's good news, isn't it?'

He tried not to wonder what they might be waiting for.

'Wonderful church you've got here,' the young man said, his smile flashing. 'Perhaps you could give me the tour? I'm the Doctor.'

The Reverend Yarwood took the man's hand and shook it. The man's manner was light enough, but there was something in his eyes that suggested he had serious matters to discuss. It never once occurred to the Reverend to think that this Doctor was another of the scared souls huddled in the church, needing his reassurance that the creatures outside would at least be deterred if not explained. In fact, the Reverend Yarwood felt more as if he should be asking the Doctor to comfort him, to make him safe again.

'The Reverend Yarwood,' Gordon said, taking the Doctor's hand in both of his. 'Gordon. I'm the minister here at St Cuthbert's.'

'And it's a lovely place,' the Doctor enthused.

Gordon took a look around the church. Ralph had

split the congregation into two parties, and both were working hard at their allotted tasks. Ralph himself was helping the first group lift the heavy wooden pews and barricade the doors with them, whilst the second scurried around looking for anything that might be used in their defence. The soldiers stood guard at the windows, muskets at the ready.

The house of God was slowly being transformed into His fortress.

Ralph looked across to Gordon and gave him a solemn nod.

'It's falling apart,' Gordon answered the Doctor's question. 'The Chapel of Ease is the only part that might stand up against those creatures outside. I'm sorry. I thought I was doing the best thing in bringing you here.'

'Nonsense,' the Doctor protested. 'Where else were we going? And this old place will still be around for a while yet. Well, sixteen years to be precise, but... Reverend Yarwood: has anything like this ever happened before?'

Gordon paused for a moment. 'I did read once of a man named Lazarus,' he answered.

The Doctor smiled.

He had led them very casually away from the work that Ralph had instigated. Perhaps he understood that the congregation would feel uncomfortable tearing up the church under the eyes of their minister, even if it was necessary. It had been Gordon who had first spotted the boat and its pursuers, standing at the pulpit about to begin. He had seen the Nor' Loch bubbling and part of him had, he was sure, hoped that it was the Apocalypse. Like Thomas before him, Gordon would have been remarkably comforted to find that his faith hadn't been misplaced all of these years.

But instead he had run out, to see what help he could give. The Lord had given him faith, but He had also given him intelligence, and Gordon doubted that God wanted him to give up either to the other. His head told him that this was an earthly tribulation, and that his congregation needed what little protection he could give.

'Will they be safe?' Gordon asked.

The Doctor looked away. 'You worry about them,' he said, with a tone that made it clear that he had someone to worry about as well.

'I'm responsible for them,' Gordon answered. 'From this life, into the next.'

'They seem to appreciate you,' the Doctor said.

He was looking across the church, at the small group hefting a pew across the doorway. Ralph was standing at its centre, a large round man with chestnut hair running all around his face. He had paused in his work for just a moment, leaning down to the tearful blonde child who was trying to cling to his leg. He gave his daughter an all-enveloping hug and kissed her forehead, and without a word made her feel that it would be all right. Gordon knew that the Doctor was thinking of Ralph jumping to Gordon's protection, and smiled gently.

'Ralph Williamson, perhaps,' Gordon said. 'But then he did marry my sister. She wouldn't expect any less.'

'They're here,' the Doctor said, 'and they're not panicking. I think you can take the credit for that.'

'Perhaps,' Gordon said. 'I think perhaps it is partly that they have long memories, too. I still sometimes think that they come here because they hope I might show myself to be one tenth the minister that their previous was. They still talk about him now as the best minister the church ever had, and the Reverend McVicar died some twelve years ago.'

The Doctor smiled. 'There's always someone to tell you the last one was twice as good as you are,' he said. 'Doesn't mean that they're right.'

Gordon gave a little sigh. 'They tell a story,' he said quietly, 'about the Reverend McVicar. He was a brave man, and he wasn't afraid of pushing himself forward if he knew it was right. Not everyone loved him for it: one man, the story says, announced that he would have gladly thrashed McVicar, if it hadn't been for his minister's coat.'

Gordon looked down at his own neat dark coat.

'The Reverend McVicar threw his coat on the ground, shouting "There lies the Minister of the West Kirk and here stands Neil McVicar, and by Yea and by Nay, sir, come on!",' Gordon told the Doctor. 'The man didn't wait to see if he meant it.'

The Doctor put a firm hand on Gordon's shoulder.

'The day's not over,' he said. 'They might be telling stories about you yet.'

The Doctor kept his eyes flicking about the church, and tried to think of the positives. McAllister's men had spread out and were actually obeying orders, rather than trying to catch sight of the creatures for themselves. Two manned the barrier at the main doors, whilst the others were covering the windows. McAllister himself stood at the pulpit and oversaw all that he surveyed. His eyes momentarily caught the Doctor's; he nodded briefly, then turned away.

The Doctor, meanwhile, ran through the options in his head. The dead rising wasn't as uncommon as all that, and his main problem in identifying the cause was that there were too many to choose from, not too few. He needed more information. So far, all he knew was that they had come out of the water and they were waiting outside. That, and they hadn't attacked the living until that first frightened soldier had fired off his musket.

Something caught the Doctor's eye.

One of the parishioners had broken off from the main group, the white-haired man called Thomas. He was walking strangely, a vacant sort of look on his face that the Doctor didn't much like. He looked to where the old man was heading, and he saw a small window and a door that the soldiers had missed, hidden by a thick curtain. Behind the window, there was a dark shadow patiently waiting.

'This Reverend McVicar,' the Doctor asked. 'Where did they bury him?'

'In the churchyard,' the Reverend Yarwood replied. 'Why?'

'Oh, no reason,' he said.

'He's come back to us!' Thomas cried out in disbelief.

The Doctor closed his eyes, briefly.

Everybody in the church turned and looked, but nobody reacted.

The Doctor launched himself over a pew and raced to intercept, but he knew he was going to be too late. So much for getting an overview of the stage before the curtains went up.

Thomas had reached the door and was already

swinging it open, and a gasp went through the church as everybody realised what he was doing.

'Prepare arms!' McAllister yelled. The Doctor didn't know if the Captain expected his men to shoot Thomas, or what was going to come through the door.

'Wait!' the Doctor yelled, unsure who at.

But Thomas stepped back, turning to the congregation with a look on his face that suggested he expected them to be just as happy as him. Standing in the doorway was a squat, dark figure with broad shoulders and a powerful build. He was still dressed in the same drab minister's coat that they had buried him in. The same coat he'd once thrown to the ground to make a point.

The Reverend McVicar had returned.

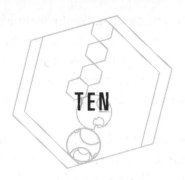

TEN

Martha hovered by the coffin trying to decide what she should do. Part of her said she should open it, but she couldn't think of any sane reason why she would want to. All the same, her hand started to stretch out to it, almost of its own accord. She turned her face away from the inevitable, as if by not seeing it she could be sure that she wasn't doing it.

'Don't touch that!'

Martha jumped, feeling a strong urge to run and run and never stop. Instead, she snatched her hand away and turned.

Alexander was there, his face filled with an anger so fierce that it might well be able to melt metal. His hands were covered with heavy leather gloves, and an apron covered him from shoulder to toe: Martha realised with a jolt that this was him dressed for surgery.

He was holding the two disembodied hands.

'How did you get out?' he asked, stepping closer.

Martha should have run, but instead she hesitated.

The older Monro entered the room through another doorway, still dressed in his everyday clothes but carrying two of the pottery batteries that he had used in her cell. They looked heavy, but such was his surprise at seeing Martha that he didn't put them down. He just stood there, staring at her. Alexander took another step forward.

'Don't just gawp,' he snapped. 'Help me catch her.'

'And what then?' Martha asked.

Alexander simply glared.

'Hold her,' he growled.

Martha looked to Monro.

'No,' the old anatomist said.

'No?'

'This isn't what we wanted, Alexander,' he said simply.

'So what did you want?' Martha asked.

Monro looked at her so sadly.

'My father was a great man,' the old man said quietly. 'He died when he still had so much he could offer. To the world: the whole world was lessened when he passed away, do you understand?'

Monro looked to the coffin on the table. Martha remembered the brass plaque: John Monro. For a moment, she thought of her own father. Leaving her mother and advertising his midlife crisis to the whole of London with the help of Annalise. What would she do, when the time finally came? Beg the Doctor to take her back and change it all? She knew she'd give anything to have him back.

Then she remembered the pale highwayman.

'Look, I know you miss your dad,' Martha said. For a moment, Monro looked like he might cry. 'But this isn't right. You know it isn't. I don't think they're even the same people they were when you bring them back. Do you?'

Monro paused, just for a moment.

'Why are you listening to her?' Alexander yelled.

He threw down the hands he was about to experiment on. As the hands dropped onto the operating table, he tugged his heavy leather gloves off, letting them fall to the floor. A moment later, Alexander was nearly on her. The look on his face almost made Martha sick: there was so much of his father's gentleness there, but the anger twisted it and made it so ugly. She took a breath and a step back, bringing her arms up to defend herself.

Alexander was hit clean in the chest by a clay battery.

He flew backwards, his body twitching as the electricity earthed itself through him. As if in sympathy, the hands lay twitching violently on the operating table. Alexander seemed to fly for several long seconds before he landed hard behind the table with a loud thump. Martha looked at Monro, but Alexander's father was just standing holding the other battery as if he expected someone else to admit that they had hit his son.

'Mr Monro?' she asked.

He blinked, twice. 'Mary,' he said, looking at her. 'He was going to hurt you. Are you all right?'

Martha looked over to the table. 'I think we should worry about your son.'

Monro just looked at her like a small child. 'My son?' he said. 'Alexander isn't my son.'

But it was too late for questions: Alexander rose silently from behind the operating table. His nose was bloody, and he was smiling a grim smile that really didn't bode well. His leather apron had swung around to one side as he'd fallen, and Alexander just casually reached out and plucked it off. It fell to the floor, revealing that his shirt had opened almost to the waist.

Martha gasped.

She could see Alexander's pale white chest. Underneath the skin around his heart, there were five lumps poking out. It was only as they flexed convulsively that she realised they were the fingertips of a hand that was growing beneath the skin. Martha took a step back; she could still run, there was no one behind her. But Alexander's father was just standing there meekly, waiting to be caught.

'Mr Monro,' she said urgently. 'It's all right. Don't be afraid. You just need to come with me, OK? It'll be all right.'

Alexander laughed coldly at that. 'Do you think you can turn him against me?'

Martha held her hand out to Monro. 'Mr Monro,' she hissed. 'Please! He's not your son.'

Monro just blinked dull-wittedly. 'I know,' he said.

'You don't understand,' Alexander said flatly. 'How could you? I didn't. You haven't looked, have you? Those hands: don't they look familiar to you?'

Martha looked at them, the two hands flapping on the floor as they tried to right themselves. Pale white hands cut off at the wrist, both with the same wart on the index fingers, each with the same pattern of scars on the fingertips. They were, she suddenly realised, the hands of someone who worked with knives every day.

'Let us show you four more,' Alexander said, holding up his own.

They were pale white hands, with a wart growing

at the base of the index finger on his left hand. Every finger had a faint etching of white scars criss-crossed across it. They were a surgeon's hands, used to working with knives every day.

Martha looked to Monro for some kind of explanation, but the old man couldn't meet her eyes. Instead, he just held up his own hands: the fingers were criss-crossed with scars, and the left index finger had a wart growing at its base.

'I am going to bring back my father,' said Alexander firmly.

'Because I miss him so very much,' said the other, older Alexander.

ELEVEN

The Doctor heard the sound of muskets cocking before he was anywhere near the door, and he knew that McAllister would give the order without hesitation. Probably even if the Doctor was in the line of fire – possibly even because. Even so, he dived forward, jumping over pews and trying very hard not to knock down parishioners as he went.

'Don't shoot!' he shouted as authoritatively as he could.

McVicar just stood there framed in the open doorway, looking straight ahead and not breathing. Even old Thomas looked like he was having second thoughts about the minister's miraculous return. He said the minister's name once, and then backed slowly away. The creature didn't even look up, just stood there blinking slowly, as if not quite sure what it wanted to do now that it was here.

'Take aim!' McAllister bellowed.

'No!' the Doctor said firmly.

He placed himself directly in front of the dead minister. The creature looked up slowly, as if seeing him from a great distance. It blinked again. Its eyes were clear and grey.

'Move out of the way,' McAllister shouted.

He ran across the room, clearly intending to drag the Doctor out of the line of fire. He did have some redeeming human features, then.

'I think it would be a better idea to shut that door,' the Doctor said, not taking his eyes from the minister. 'Don't you?'

McAllister didn't say anything, but suddenly all eyes turned to the door that was still hanging open. Through it, they could see the churchyard, filled with hundreds of pale, blank-eyed figures. They just stood there, swaying, as if they were waiting for McVicar to do something on their behalf. Perhaps they were, the Doctor considered: perhaps he was an envoy of some sort. A negotiator.

The churchyard was getting fuller. Some of the creatures out there were digging up the ground with their bare hands. This wasn't caused by anything in the waters in the Loch, the Doctor decided, unless they had seeped through into the churchyard.

The Reverend Yarwood edged quickly around the creature and slammed the door shut, taking a key from his robes and locking it. He couldn't help but peer out of the small window at the mass of bodies waiting outside. He looked over to the Doctor nervously. McAllister scowled and looked to his men; he motioned for one to join him, putting a ring of armed men around McVicar. The Doctor ignored him and held his hand out to the creature.

'Can you hear me?' he asked.

The eyes seemed to flicker.

'I'm the Doctor,' he pressed on. 'I can help you.'

The Doctor could feel the silence pressing down on him. Everybody in that little tumbledown church was staring at him, waiting for something to happen. They all stood perfectly still, as if afraid that even the slightest movement might suddenly spark off a murderous rampage. But the creature had come in here for something, and it had come in alone: if the walking dead had just wanted to kill, they would have attacked en masse and torn the church apart with their bare hands.

What was this one looking for, he wondered.

'Are you Gelth?' the Doctor tried. Still McVicar looked at him blankly. 'All right then, not Gelth. That's good: you don't seem very Gelthish, and I don't remember there being a rift in Edinburgh. So… just hold very still, this won't hurt a bit.'

The Doctor reached inside his jacket and very slowly pulled out his sonic screwdriver. The creature didn't react, but McAllister gave him a questioning look. Behind them, the blonde girl gave a little frightened gasp and buried her face in Ralph Williamson's side. The Doctor smiled as charmingly as he could manage, and flicked the sonic screwdriver on: its warbling cry filled the church, and there was a sharp intake of breath from the congregation.

The Doctor raised his eyebrows at what he was seeing.

'Now that's interesting,' he said to himself.

'What?' McAllister asked.

'He's dead,' the Doctor announced.

'He died twelve years ago, Doctor,' the Reverend Yarwood said helpfully.

'No, I mean he's dead,' the Doctor said, shaking his head. 'Just a normal dead body. No abnormal readings whatsoever.'

'Except that it's walking,' McAllister countered.

'Yes.' The Doctor flashed him a smile. 'Odd, isn't it?'

McAllister scowled, but the Doctor concentrated on his sonic screwdriver as the rest of the church just watched him. He needed to be quick. So far the creature hadn't decided that it wanted more of a look around: if it did, he wasn't sure that he could stop McAllister from having his men shoot it. It hadn't been the best thing to do when they were outside and could run. Inside, it would be fatal.

'Aha!' the Doctor cried suddenly.

'What?' McAllister asked again. His patience was wearing thin.

'That's why I wasn't picking anything up,' the Doctor explained, waving the screwdriver over the creature again. 'It's static electricity. The sonic screwdriver doesn't automatically look for static.'

'Why not?' McAllister snapped.

'Well, because it's sonic,' the Doctor answered. 'And static's static.'

Sometimes, people did ask stupid questions.

'This creature's riddled with it,' the Doctor said. 'And in much higher concentrations than you normally get in humans. It's a good thing you haven't got a nylon carpet in here.'

'The Reverend Neil McVicar,' the Reverend Yarwood said.

The Doctor looked up at him.

'You said "this creature",' the Reverend Yarwood said sternly. 'He is not a creature. He was a man, and a minister in this church. He is not a creature.'

'I'm sorry,' the Doctor said.

And then he went back to the screwdriver.

'The whole body is flooded with static, that's what's keeping it…' The Doctor paused for a moment, glancing at the Reverend Yarwood. 'That's what's keeping him moving. It's flowing all through his central nervous system, but there seems to be an unusual concentration of it.'

The Doctor waved the sonic screwdriver all over the creature's body, tracing the flow of the static. As he brought it up to the chest, he reached out carefully and flicked open the long black coat it was wearing. Beneath it, the shirt had been torn and was hanging open in flaps.

'Here,' the Doctor said, pointing at the heart.

Directly over it sat what seemed to be a human hand.

The Reverend Yarwood stood next to Captain McAllister, his back to the door. He didn't want to have to look out of that window again and see what the poor souls outside his church were doing to the graveyard. Instead, he stood facing his illustrious predecessor's back, the Doctor's naked scientific curiosity and his congregation. He felt he should be among his parishioners, not addressing them on high from the pulpit but here on the ground with them. One or two were looking at McVicar or the soldiers, but most were looking to him. They wanted him to tell them what was happening, and how they could be saved from it.

'Don't move,' the Doctor said, holding up his hand. 'It's a hand. It looks like a human hand. And it's what's making the bodies walk. I wonder why?'

The Reverend Yarwood felt queasy.

'What do they want?' Captain McAllister asked.

'Hold on,' the Doctor checked his wand again. 'Oh, it doesn't say.' He glared at the Captain.

'Then I shall have to assume they have hostile intentions,' McAllister said calmly. 'Step aside or be shot down with it.'

The Doctor's head snapped up at that.

'Don't you understand, McAllister?' he said. 'Look at it. Him. He's just standing there. He's not attacking; he's not hurting any one of us. He isn't interested. The only thing that made them attack before was that your men opened fire on them. They fought back to protect themselves. They obviously didn't come here to attack us, so they must want something else. If we can find out what it is and give it to them... nobody else has to die today, Captain.'

'And what if the price is too high?' McAllister countered.

The Reverend Yarwood could see his congregation looking to him, waiting for him to throw down his coat and challenge both men to settle it by fighting him. The Reverend kept his coat firmly buttoned up, but that didn't mean that he would let this go on any longer.

'Captain McAllister,' he said firmly. 'Ask your men to lay down their arms. I will not have them firing muskets on this sacred ground. Not until lives are at risk.'

'Lives *are* at risk!' McAllister rounded on him, spittle flying. 'What do you think that is standing there? They killed my man. They *killed* my man!'

'I am sorry,' the Reverend Yarwood said, as calmly as he could.

Suddenly, every member of the congregation felt something that made them jump. Even the Doctor, calm and rational as he was, took a step backwards. He put his arms in the air and ordered the soldiers not to open fire. They managed to hold their trigger fingers for that moment, possibly because their Captain was momentarily too busy trying to move to give the order.

McVicar turned on his heel.

'Doctor?' the Reverend Yarwood asked.

McVicar was standing only inches from him: if he had been breathing, the Reverend would have been able to feel it on his face. Instead, he could just feel the chill coming from the minister's pale grey flesh.

'Of course!' the Doctor cried.

Yarwood was pleased that at least one of them was happy.

'There are more hands than there are bodies in the Loch,' the Doctor was saying. The Reverend Yarwood was staring deep into McVicar's grey eyes. 'They need more bodies, and we led them right here.'

McVicar pushed by Yarwood without even noticing him, walking back towards the door he had come in by. The soldier guarding the door didn't let out a sound but, as Yarwood spun around, he saw that the man had his musket raised.

'No, don't stop him!' the Doctor shouted. 'He's just going back out to join his friends. As long as they're not being attacked, they don't care about the living, see? They only want the dead.'

'I feel profoundly comforted,' McAllister snapped.

The soldier on the door wasn't moving. The Reverend Yarwood could see his finger shaking as it hovered over the trigger. He knew that he was standing so close to McVicar that he might well get hit himself. Then he remembered the important thing.

'I locked the door!' he cried out.

The key was in his hand, but McAllister snatched it away.

'Stay back!' the soldier cried.

McVicar didn't listen: why would he?

'Wait!' the Doctor shouted.

But the Reverend Yarwood could see the soldier squeezing the trigger.

So he closed his eyes.

McAllister saw that Howkins' nerve had given way. There was a cold sweat on his brow, and his eyes were two black pinpricks in his face. There were only two options: either he could be brought down, or he could be given his head. One would definitely lose him a soldier, but the other might let the young boy steady himself and come back. Either way, there was no point in giving an order which Howkins wouldn't obey in this state. That would only leave McAllister looking weak.

The Captain decided then that he would let Howkins shoot, and see if he could be calmed once the corpse was safely dead again. After all, what loss was it to him?

'Wait!' the prisoner shouted.

That blue-tipped wand was in his hand again, and suddenly McAllister found his ears aching. He closed his eyes in pain and thought how, in less enlightened times, the prisoner would have been called a witch and safely douked in the Nor' Loch by now. Perhaps there was something to be said for the old ways after all.

The earache abruptly passed and, as McAllister opened his eyes, he saw the pale corpse suddenly crumple to the floor. A murmur somewhere between relief and dismay travelled through the congregation, and McAllister knew that it was time to act. He stepped forward and raised his arms authoritatively.

'Don't trouble yourselves,' he barked. 'You are safe now.'

He nodded to his men to ready themselves. Just in case the churchgoers weren't as comforted by that thought as they should have been.

The prisoner was on the floor by the time McAllister turned again, kneeling by the corpse. Suddenly, it was nothing more than another fallen body, ready to be returned to the earth from which it had come. This was a strange day indeed, and McAllister wasn't looking forward to having to explain it to the Lord Provost. Perhaps some kind of mass delusion could be blamed. The townsfolk would believe that if it made life easier for them.

'It's all right,' the prisoner was saying.

In his hands, he cupped something small and trembling. The hand's fingers twitched convulsively, but it didn't make any move to escape. McAllister could see dusty flesh under its sharp nails, where it had evidently been clinging tight to the minister's dead chest. The Captain considered knocking it from the Doctor's grip and grinding it under his boot, but he didn't. Until it proved itself still a threat.

'See?' the prisoner was saying. 'It's just like a friendly tarantula. No trouble at all.'

'We should move the Reverend McVicar's body to a more suitable place,' the bald minister said. 'Is it safe?'

'Perfectly,' the prisoner answered. 'Without this little fellow.'

The Reverend nodded, and McAllister stood back as Yarwood called to two of the parishioners to help move the body. One was the old man who had originally opened the door; someone that McAllister would need to talk to once this was all over. The minister simply laid a hand on the man's arm and said something McAllister didn't hear. The old man nodded, and then the three of them carefully lifted the body and carried it away.

The prisoner held the twitching hand, their fingers interlocking as if they were young lovers. His wand was in his free hand, pointing it at the creature and reading the report through a pair of thick-rimmed spectacles.

McAllister looked around the church, and saw that everybody was watching the prisoner, even his own men. He stepped forward and cleared his throat meaningfully.

'Don't worry, Captain,' the prisoner said. 'It isn't hurt. The sonic screwdriver shocked it into letting go, but can't do it any real harm. They're not compatible.'

'One is sonic, and the other static,' McAllister repeated.

'Exactly.'

McAllister nodded. 'So the wand is no use to us as a weapon,' he said.

The prisoner gave him a dark look. 'That's why I carry it,' he answered.

Then he went back to examining the hand and his wand, pulling his spectacles down so that he could peer over the top of them.

'Strange,' he muttered to himself. 'It's not really a hand at all: it's some kind of organic machine. Looks like it can reproduce asexually – which explains why there's so many of them. There's some kind of deep level programming in here, but it's all messed—'

There was a loud thud from the door behind them.

'What was that?' asked a voice from the congregation.

McAllister spun around, but the window beside the door was completely blocked by something outside. Several somethings. More deep thuds began to sound out from the door, and the stonework of the walls started to scrape and whine as the creatures outside tried to pull the stones out one by one. He had no idea how many of the things there might be out there by now: St Cuthbert's had been here since long before McAllister's father had been born, and its churchyard was well stocked.

'They're trying to get in,' McAllister said.

'Ah,' said the prisoner. 'That might be my fault. If they know that I've disconnected this one from its host... It could be the same protective instinct that made them attack your men.'

McAllister looked around the church one last time. The walls were old and crumbling, and it had been in need of rebuilding for several years now. If he managed to escape, he might even mention that to the Lord Provost. But it was no fortress now, and he knew there was no way that they would keep out a determined army of indefinite numbers for very long. The parishioners were starting to get twitchy. Presumably, they'd come to the same conclusion as he had, but knew there was nowhere safer for them to run to.

'Is there a crypt under the church?' McAllister shouted.

No one answered.

Very well.

'Howkins,' he said, spinning back to the nervous

soldier by the door. He looked back guiltily, obviously considering his chances if he ran. 'You're the youngest married man in the guard, yes? What's her name?'

'Sir?'

'Your wife, Howkins.'

'Betty, sir,' Howkins said.

The soldier was barely more than a boy, and he kept twitching every time the sound of a blow hit the wall behind him. Given time, he would make a brave soldier, McAllister was sure. He had moulded worse than that in his time. He thought briefly of his own Rosalie waiting for him in their turnpike house on Fleshmarket Close. But she had always known this day might come, and there was nothing to say to make it any easier for her.

'When the enemy gains entry,' McAllister said firmly, 'you will lead these civilians away from the church. Their safety is your responsibility, do you understand? Once they are safe, you will go home to your wife and tell her you love her.'

'But the creatures—' Howkins stammered.

'The enemy will be held in the church,' McAllister shouted, a general order for the rest of his men. They watched him pale-faced, and nodded their understanding. 'For as long as is possible, anyhow.'

Howkins swallowed. Something in his eyes made McAllister sure that the soldier understood exactly what he had just been given: a life, children and happiness – exactly what the rest of them were sacrificing so that the civilians could keep theirs.

'There is another option,' the prisoner said, stepping forwards.

McAllister looked at him.

'I can go out there and show them that the hand is all right.'

'They'll tear you apart,' McAllister said.

'They only seem to attack in self-defence,' the prisoner said. 'And if they don't, I don't think I'd stand any less of a chance out there than I would in here. You should at least let me try.'

McAllister looked the prisoner up and down. He remembered his earlier assessment of him, that he had seen military service somewhere in his life. Obviously, they had trained him as well as McAllister's old sergeant had trained him. McAllister nodded, and turned to Howkins.

'Open the door,' he said, handing Howkins the minister's key. 'As we pass through, you will close and lock it again. If we don't come back, my previous orders still stand.'

'There's no reason for you to come as well,' the prisoner said. 'You should stay with your men.'

McAllister just stood by his side.

'You are my prisoner,' McAllister reminded him.

'It is my duty to keep you safe until the Lord Provost decides that we can hang you.'

The prisoner smiled.

'Well, when you put it like that…'

'Open the door,' ordered McAllister.

And they stepped out.

TWELVE

'I found it,' Monro told Martha. 'A long time ago. It did not look like my hand then. It was different: mechanical, less human. I found it.'

He remembered it, just as he knew his other self would. Thirty years previously, a brewster selling her ales on the Closes that bordered the Loch had brought it to him. It had not looked like a hand at all, the brewster told him, not until she had picked it up and it had shifted. Suddenly, it had become a sleek blackened steel five-digit shape. The brewster had been paid for her trouble, and Monro had begun to study the strange hand.

'As I picked it up,' he said, hearing his younger self's impatient tutting, 'its nails dug into me, drawing blood. I fainted clean away. When my wife found me, the hand had released me. When I held it again, it was the mirror of my own.'

'We don't need to tell her this,' his twin said sharply.

Not for the first time, Monro wished that whatever strange process had created his twin had also left him with the ability to read his mind. Would he find the mirror of his own thoughts there as well? The excitement that his plan was so nearly complete, and that father would soon be with him. The desire to talk and delay that moment as long as possible, because of the nagging fear that it would go wrong. That it was already wrong, much more wrong than anything could ever be?

'It responded to electricity,' he continued, ignoring his younger twin. 'Specifically in its static form.'

'Aren't they both the same thing?' she asked.

Poor thing. Perhaps it was foolish to expect a woman to understand the intricacies of science.

'I began experimenting,' he told her. 'Testing the hand's responses to the electricity. At first, it seemed to have a detrimental effect, but soon there were surprising results. On contact with the current, the hand split itself in two, each a perfect copy of the other. On my next experiment, one attached itself to my leg, and nothing I could do would make it release.'

His poor Isabella. How scared she had been.

How scared he had been.

The first day, he had told himself that nothing had happened and tried to keep it from his wife. Every moment that passed, the lump on his leg seemed to grow larger by degrees. There was no hiding it from her, and he had been forced to confess it all. She had kissed his forehead, and told him they would do whatever it took.

By the morning, they had been parents.

'What happened?' Martha asked him.

His other self replied.

'I was born from his thigh,' his young face sneered. 'Twice born, like Dionysus himself. With all my father's knowledge up until we were separated, and a new young life to put it to use again.'

'And you want to do that to your father?' the woman asked.

'You have seen the hands' other properties,' Alexander said. 'We intend to reanimate our father and, once he is living, we can use the hand a second time to copy him. He will be returned to use as a babe in arms, ready to resume his work the moment he can talk.'

The woman's distaste was plain to see.

'Please,' Monro said to her. 'Please. You are young still. Don't think any less of me: there are still so many things I wanted to do. Now I have another life to do them with. How could I deny my father the same blessing?'

She shook her head.

'Another life? Well, maybe.' She gave his other self a look of pure disdain. 'But yours? He might look like you, but he's only got your memories up to a point, hasn't he? Can you tell me what he's thinking now?'

Monro looked at his younger self. The sneer was still on his face, and he was edging ever closer to where Martha stood. She stood at the edge of the stage, alone and vulnerable. It made him automatically think of her as a student, to feel the need to explain how it worked until she brightened with the understanding.

He could only hope his other self felt the same.

'He's just a copy,' she said. So reasonably. 'He's not you. He might still be here when you go, but will that make any difference?'

Monro simply bit his lip.

Martha could see Monro thinking about what she was saying, could see him agreeing. She had to stop herself from holding out her hand to him and telling him to come on and stop being silly. Partly because she didn't want to break the faint hold she had on him, and partly because it would have brought her closer to Alexander. She didn't trust him not to grab her and tie her to the operating table. There was something there in his eyes: there was no way the two men were the same.

'Your dad wouldn't thank you for this,' Martha said.

Just for a moment, she thought she might have him.

Suddenly, Alexander moved. He didn't come for her, but she jumped nonetheless and found herself looking for the nearest exit. Instead, he had suddenly fallen to his knees, grabbing the two disembodied hands that were scuttling around his feet. He held them aloft, struggling like two crabs trying to avoid the cooking pot.

'If you are going to stop us, then stop us,' Alexander growled at her. 'If you are going to run and bring the bailies, then do it. But we have work to be doing, and no more time for your prattling. Are you going to assist, *father*, or are you not?'

Monro shuddered at the harsh tones of Alexander's voice. He didn't look up, didn't catch Martha's eye. Instead he shuffled over to the coffin on the table, and started to pull off the wet wooden lid.

'Wait!' Martha called.

Alexander just leered at her.

'My father was a great man,' he said sternly. 'You will thank us when you meet him.'

And he turned away, back to his coffin.

Martha wondered what to do. She knew that playing Frankenstein in the middle of the afternoon wasn't going to turn out well, but there was only one of her, and two of him. The only advantage she had was that they didn't think she had any advantage at all. That was usually enough for the Doctor. Perhaps it would work just as well for her?

'Alexander,' she said.

Monro looked up, but Alexander didn't turn. Instead, he started shaking his arms as if trying to dislodge something. Martha could see the two disembodied hands he held, fingers locked tight into his: they were holding on and they weren't going to let go.

'Alexander?' she echoed.

He spun around then, a look of panic on his face.

'Something has—'

Alexander broke off as the fingers in his chest suddenly twitched. He gave a loud scream, and Martha watched as he dropped to his knees, his own fingers hit by a convulsive spasm. The two extra hands he held still clung on tight, twitching and vibrating and digging their nails in so far as to draw little beads of blood. Monro abandoned the coffin and ran to his clone's side.

'Alexander? What is it?' he asked.

Alexander just shouted again.

'What's that noise?' asked Martha.

She could hear it, just at the edges of perception: a low, bass rumble that was shaking the floor beneath her. She looked around, but the whole room was vibrating now and it was impossible to judge just where the sound was coming from. It sounded like a tidal wave was sweeping its way through the building. The Doctor had said the Castle was built on an old volcano – was it erupting after all this time? Surely that was something even the Doctor would have thought to mention.

The hairs on the back of her neck started to rise, and Martha managed to get a bearing on where the sound was coming from. There was no way that this was going to be good.

'Mr Monro,' she said cautiously.

Monro turned to look at her. His mouth fell open.

The doors burst open.

Martha turned around as fast as she could, but they were already at her ankles before she even registered what they were.

Hands scuttled all over the floor, all over the walls, over the seats and into the auditorium. Hundreds of them, maybe even thousands. Some of them had to be the ones from the cell she had been kept in, but not all of them surely. The room just wasn't that big. Even the lecture theatre seemed too small to contain the horde of hands that was pouring through the doorway and rushing towards her.

And past her.

Monro gave a scream.

Martha spun back again, all thoughts of escape forgotten: the two Alexander Monros needed her help. The hands were pretty much ignoring the elder but, as they fought and flurried to reach the younger, many accidentally struck him just as hard as if they'd meant it. The old man barely seemed to notice. Instead he clawed and pulled at the hands, crying out as they attached themselves to his clone. Alexander was fast disappearing beneath a mass of writhing grey flesh.

Martha knew there was nothing they could do: even as Monro managed to get one hand to release its grip, another five had already clung tight. Alexander himself didn't even seem to be struggling, but then he had that extra hand buried in his chest – had it somehow been preparing him for this moment? It didn't matter: Martha jumped forward and grabbed hold of Monro's arm, pulling him sharply away.

'We've got to go,' Martha shouted.

'But—' the old anatomist tried to argue.

'Now!'

And Martha pulled him again, away from the door at the far end of the auditorium and towards the side entrance they had brought the coffin in from. She could only hope that there was another way out from back there, and that it was one that wasn't already blocked by more hands scrabbling towards them. At least Monro seemed to realise the inevitable, and gave up trying to pull away from her. He gave one last look over his shoulder at the ball of flesh that had buried Alexander, and then he bolted for the door.

Martha paused only to scoop up a stray hand, and then ran.

Its fingers flexed as she ran.

The hands threw themselves at the loci, acting on pure animal instinct and nothing more. Fingers clutched at fingers, and hands grabbed wrists, and slowly the mess of writhing digits began to take the shape of something else. As each hand touched another, tendrils of electricity and intelligence reached out and joined. Slowly, the intelligence was taking shape. The understanding that the hands had been damaged – were still damaged – began to emerge. The knowledge that in their confusion they had each been attaching themselves to a different loci, when they should have been merging and joining around a single whole.

Then the pain, and the sudden clarity.

The sonic burst that had repaired them.

It took a few minutes for the emerging intelligence to begin to distinguish between what was inside itself and what was out. It felt the wood under its skin, and it felt the cold damp air, but it didn't quite understand yet that these were things that weren't a part of it. It felt the sparking panic of the loci suddenly subsumed under the creature's growing awareness. Of itself, as one.

As its understanding grew, it began to sense those hands that were still outside of itself, and called them all to it. It knew it could only reach the stage of truly knowing what it was once it had the critical mass that every hand could provide. It also knew that it was not alone in the room, that there two others in the room that weren't it. It felt, as one of them reached down and grabbed a struggling hand from the floor and then ran from the room.

It didn't yet know itself, but it found that it could know anger.

So it grew legs and gave chase.

THIRTEEN

The Doctor stepped out very slowly and calmly, holding the hand out in front of him like he was waiting for someone to take it and shake it. The creatures that had been attacking the door and the walls all stood back the instant they saw the hand. It was as if an invisible line had been drawn around the hand, the Doctor and Captain McAllister that none of them wanted to cross. The Doctor glanced back briefly at McAllister, but the soldier kept his face impassive.

'Stay close,' the Doctor whispered.

'Should I?' McAllister asked blithely.

The Doctor took another step forward, his trainers sinking into the soft ground. The majority of the creatures surrounding them had come up from the bottom of the Loch, and the water was still dripping from them, turning the earth into mud. The Doctor looked up at the gloomy clouds above. It didn't look like the grass was going to get the chance to dry out any time soon.

'Have you seen what they've done to the church?' McAllister whispered.

The Doctor took a quick glance behind him: the wooden door had been splintered and shredded by long sharp nails scratching across it, but it was the brickwork that was the most shocking. Whole bricks had been torn out of the wall, or else just crumbled to dust where they sat. Whatever else they were, these creatures were strong. If they decided to take a dislike to them now, there was no chance that the Doctor or McAllister would make it back inside.

'They must not reach the Castle,' McAllister said firmly.

The Doctor glanced up at the Castle Rock, looming up to their left over the dull grey mirror of the Loch. It looked so permanent, so impregnable. He estimated it would take the creatures a good few minutes before they could breach the defences and get at those inside. If they decided that was what they wanted to do.

'Does it look like they want to?' the Doctor asked.

'I have my duty,' McAllister answered.

The Doctor tutted loudly.

'At least you didn't bring a musket,' he said.

'The musket isn't a close-quarters weapon,' was all McAllister would say.

The Doctor didn't look at him: he kept his eyes on the rapt audience that was standing, watching him. As he stepped away from the church, the creatures moved in around him, never coming close enough to touch him. They were an eclectic mix, to be certain: redcoats in fading uniforms, highlanders in weed-soaked kilts, wryters from all through the ages with lank hair sticking to their sunken-eyed skulls, and a lord in his finery who could have been a member of the Slitheen family in disguise. Each had a single hand clutching to their breast that was the mirror to the one twitching groggily in the Doctor's own.

'This can't be what you were made for,' the Doctor told them. 'This is just you trying to get out of the Loch. So what are you here for? What were you meant to do? If you tell me, I can help.'

The creatures looked at him, blank eyed.

'They're dead,' McAllister said. 'They can't talk.'

The Doctor looked down sadly.

'Dead men tell no tales, eh, McAllister?' he said.

And he reached into his jacket pocket.

The prisoner – the Doctor – simply stood in the centre of the ring of the walking dead, holding that bodiless hand in his and looking into each face as if it was someone important to him. Each face looked back blankly, grey skin and grey eyes, no life in them. McAllister saw them differently: there were no individuals in that crowd, just a mass of men that he might need to fight his way through. He eyed them cautiously, weighing up where the crowd was thinnest and judging which of the creatures might be stronger than its neighbour. Without turning, he was acutely aware that every one of them was following the Doctor away from the church. He hoped that Howkins had taken note and was already leading the civilians away.

They had moved further into the churchyard – perhaps the Doctor had the same thought as him and wanted to get the creatures away from the church, but it was a dispiriting sight that met them. The churchyard was dotted with holes, piles of earth thrown up wherever a hole wasn't, and here and there a headstone tumbled. There were more of the creatures than there had been on the other side of the Loch, and it wasn't hard to imagine where they had come from.

The Doctor pulled his wand from his pocket, and started waving it at each of the creatures in turn. At one point, he put it into his mouth to free a hand to pull his spectacles from his pocket, only to tear them off again as if he could not believe what they had revealed to his eyes. McAllister just let him do what he would: he himself was considering whether light artillery might succeed where muskets had failed, and how he might communicate his need to the Castle.

'Benjamin Franklin,' the Doctor said suddenly.

McAllister felt his heart jump, but kept his body neutral. It wasn't exactly a secret that the colonial statesman had visited Edinburgh, but neither was it common knowledge what he had done whilst here. Certainly McAllister didn't know, even though the Lord Provost had entrusted it to him personally to see that Franklin had a stagecoach to take him back to London again. It was well known that Franklin wasn't simply in London to bring the city news of the colonies: fifty years earlier, Scotland might have laughed at the English for entertaining the eccentric spy. Now their fates were entwined, and Edinburgh became just another piece in a complicated chess game.

McAllister had to be suspicious of the prisoner's interest in their American visitor.

'Benjamin Franklin!' the prisoner cried again, slapping his forehead.

'Is that intended as an accusation?' McAllister asked coldly.

The prisoner thrust his wand and his spectacles back into the same pocket, and when his hand reappeared it was holding something that looked like a small purple purse. He looked briefly from the purse to the disembodied hand he was holding, and then thrust the hand in McAllister's direction without preamble.

'Hold this, will you?'

McAllister found, to his wide-eyed amazement, that he took the hand from the Doctor without complaining. It felt cold against his skin: cold and clammy like wet marble. It was hard to credit that it was even alive, and yet it flexed its fingers and scratched its nails against his palm as he held it. For just a moment, the truth of what was happening threatened to overpower him: here he was, standing in a churchyard hoping to protect Edinburgh from the risen dead. He took a breath, and the moment passed. He had his duty, and his duty was first and foremost to not feel afraid.

He held the hand, and looked up at the Doctor. He was stretching the purse between his two hands, and each time he let go with one it would snap loudly back into the other. Without warning, he raised the purse to his lips and started to blow into it: it inflated squeakily, reminding McAllister of nothing more or less than a sheep's bladder. The Doctor waggled his eyebrows as he blew, and then whipped the ball from his mouth and tied a knot in the free end.

'Catch,' the Doctor said.

He batted the purple ball, and it bobbed in the air until McAllister caught it in surprise. It was only a moment later that he realised he was no longer holding the hand, but as he looked up he saw that the Doctor had it again.

'Just rub that against your head, would you?' he asked.

For no reason that he could fathom, McAllister found himself obeying. All he could think, as he rubbed the ball against his wiry hair, was that he hoped his men had evacuated the church: he would hate to think that any of them might be watching him doing this.

The Doctor, meanwhile, pointed at the hand he was holding.

'This,' he said simply, 'is a piece of snake.'

McAllister stood there, rubbing the ball against his head as the creatures surrounded them in silence and watching the hand shake itself on the Doctor's palm. Of all the things it was, a snake was not the first that would have come to mind.

'A snake,' he echoed.

The Doctor smiled boyishly.

'He was an amazing chap was Benjamin Franklin,' the Doctor said. McAllister noted that he was talking in the past tense, and wondered how long ago the two had known each other. 'A polymath, for a start. Which is impressive, if you're... you know, impressed by that kind of thing. And he invented things – invented things left, right and centre, did old Benjamin.'

McAllister stopped rubbing the ball against his head.

He frowned.

'But he was also a cartoonist,' the Doctor carried on regardless, reaching out and plucking the ball from McAllister's hands. 'He drew a cartoon called *Unite or Die*: pretty simple, just a snake cut up into a few pieces. I don't think Michelangelo was worried, but it got the point across. They used it to convince the colonies to unite against British rule.'

He pointed at the hand in his.

'This,' he said, handing it the ball, 'is a piece of snake.'

The hand leant back on the stump that was its wrist and took the ball in its fingers, closing them around the knot so tightly that the taut skin squeaked. As soon as the fingers touched that thin skin, the hairs that ran down its back stood on end and the grey flesh seemed to flicker with blue sparks. The Doctor seemed to have been expecting as much, and already had his wand in his hand again: it squealed briefly, and then cast its blue light in silence. The Doctor glanced up at McAllister.

'Wonderful stuff, static electricity,' he said. 'You wouldn't believe some of the things it can do.'

The hand twitched furiously in the Doctor's palm, digging its sharp fingers so hard into the ball it held that it suddenly burst with a loud pop. The Doctor simply smiled, as if indulging a child. The hand twisted and turned, wrapping itself in the flapping remains of the ball as if it was trying to clothe itself, and then suddenly it froze. Its fingers stretched to their full length, and the stump of its wrist pointed straight up into the air.

'And what has it done now?' McAllister asked grimly.

The Doctor merely smiled.

'Unite or die,' he said.

The hand gave a little shudder, and then in one movement it hopped from the Doctor's palm and onto the mud below. The Doctor looked to McAllister with a parental smile on his face, but McAllister was too busy watching the ring of creatures that surrounded them. He remembered how the Young Pretender's supporters had united, and what it had meant for Edinburgh as they had.

But it was too late for qualms: the little hand reached the leg of the nearest of the creatures to it, a young girl in an apron and headscarf. It clung onto her long, wet skirts with its sharp nails and scurried up her leg like a squirrel. If the girl had been alive, McAllister had no doubt that she would have been screaming. Instead, she stood in silence as the hand reached her chest, and touched the fingers of the hand that was already resting there. It was a tender caress for just a moment.

There was a brief spark, so brief that McAllister couldn't swear he hadn't imagined it. But if he had, then he would need to find some other explanation for the fact that there was only one hand clinging to the serving girl's heart. A hand that seemed almost double the size of the one that had been there before. What had the Doctor done?

The hand on the girl's chest twitched, and dropped to the floor.

Seconds later, so did the girl.

The ground around her was wet enough that, when she fell, she sank a little way into it. It wasn't as if she had fallen, or even died there and then: she fell with such force, landed without any semblance of grace, that there was no mistaking the fact that she had been dead long before she fell. All the same, McAllister couldn't help but see his own daughter lying there on the ground, the wet grass brushing against grey flesh.

The hand had already climbed another leg.

Soon another body fell.

'What is this?' McAllister asked.

The hands were all starting to wake up – somehow, without word or sign, they all knew what the Doctor had taught the first. They abandoned their host bodies to fall in the dirt as they all leapt and clawed together, two becoming four as four became eight and eight became sixteen. Soon there was a multitude of hands all running across the churchyard trying to find each other, each new addition increasing the size of the original until the smallest was the size of a decent hunting dog. Still they raced and bumped and grew. McAllister realised that they were gradually moving away from the church and closer to the Loch, shedding their hosts as they did so.

'What *is* this?' he demanded.

The Doctor looked at him, wide-eyed and excited.

'The hands aren't creatures in their own right,' he said. 'They're cells. Individual parts of something bigger. There's an instruction buried deep inside them to cling to each other, combine until they eventually become something bigger. But they were broken, and they'd got it into their heads that they should cling to the dead and get them up and about instead. So I fixed them. Now we get to see what they really are.'

'And what will that be?' McAllister asked.

The Doctor smiled that boyish smile again.

'I have absolutely no idea,' he said.

Now four creatures the size of dogs were pushing

through the trees and heading back to the murky waters of the Nor' Loch. As the four paired off, electricity crackled and suddenly there were two bears dipping into the water and pushing away from the shore. McAllister and the Doctor watched them go. The church was safe. The creatures were heading across the water towards the Castle.

'Will it be friendly?' McAllister asked.

The smile disappeared from the Doctor's face.

'We should follow them,' he said, 'shouldn't we?'

McAllister was already running: he remembered where their raft had been abandoned, and hoped fervently that the creatures hadn't scuttled it before massing on the church. He could see the wake of the bear-creatures as they swam through the brackish waters. They were already some yards from the shore, and McAllister was still some yards behind them. There could be no doubt of their destination.

'A colonial revolution?' McAllister said as they ran.

'Forget I said that,' the Doctor answered.

And they ran.

FOURTEEN

Martha ran, clutching onto Monro's hand with one hand, and holding what she knew was also Monro's hand with the other.

The doorway at the back of the stage led around to the corridor she had walked down, and there were still hands scuttling and scurrying down it but not so many that it was impossible to escape. The hand she was clutching struggled and fought, wanting to join the rest of them, but she clung on tight. She wasn't going to let it go easily: the Doctor would need to see it if he was going to work out exactly was going on here and stop it.

Monro was panting hard behind her, his free hand pressed to his chest.

'Leave me,' he told her.

Martha kept pulling him along. She'd heard that line in films more than once, and knew where it led. No: they would both escape the Surgeon's Hall, or they'd face the monster together. Alexander. Not the monster. Somewhere inside all those hands, Alexander was still there. The same man who was panting and puffing behind her, except not the same man as well. She'd grown up with the idea of cloning thanks to Dolly the Sheep: what must it be like for Monro, having seemingly discovered it out of the blue?

'When we get outside,' Martha called over her shoulder, 'we're going to keep running, OK? We're going to have to get to the Castle, only I don't know where I am so you're going to have to lead the way. All right?'

Monro didn't answer immediately, and Martha risked a quick look over her shoulder. The old anatomist was starting to go very red in the face, a purpley-bruisy kind of red, but he was nodding as he fought for breath.

Martha wondered just how long he could keep up this kind of pace. Maybe they'd be lucky: maybe the thing that had once been Alexander wouldn't be interested in chasing them. Because that was always how things had gone since she met the Doctor...

'If you start to feel shooting pains going up and

down your arms, you tell me, OK?' Martha said, and pulled Monro onwards.

The corridor was empty of hands now. They ran past the hidden door in the wall, which had been ripped from its hinges by what Martha assumed was the combined strength of hundreds of the little hands. She glanced behind her again, but this time not at Monro. There were a few hands behind them, skidding to a halt and trembling as if suddenly unsure of where they had been going in such a hurry. Perhaps they had just changed their minds about becoming one massive creature.

She could hear the heavy footfalls of something following them.

Something gigantic.

'Can we lock the door?' Martha asked.

'The door?' Monro panted.

'The front door! Have you got a key?'

Monro suddenly stopped running.

'I don't...' he panted. 'I can't... He wouldn't hurt me. It's me, don't you understand? I wouldn't hurt anyone!'

Martha's heart did a little quick-step in her chest, and she gave Monro's hand a gentle squeeze. For just a moment, she saw the poor frightened child who just wanted his father back to look after him.

'He's not you,' Martha said gently. 'He's just a bad

copy, that's all. And at the minute, he's not even that. He's just whatever these hands are. But I've got this friend, and if anyone can bring Alexander back, it's him. But we've got to get to him first. We can't stand around here. OK?'

The hands in the corridor suddenly turned and started to run towards Martha and Monro. She saw them coming, but Monro still wasn't running and so neither was she. They would both escape the Surgeon's Hall, or they'd face the monster together, and that was just the end of it. The sound of the footsteps was growing nearer, shaking the floor as if a herd of elephants was giving chase. Martha gave Monro a smile.

There was a loud roar behind them.

Martha saw the fear flash in Monro's eyes, and suddenly they were running again. The door was just ahead of them, closed but hopefully unlocked. Looking over her shoulder, Martha saw the other end of the corridor: a large mass of grey flesh filled it from floor to ceiling, almost like a man with indistinct legs, arms and even a head. The only things that she could make out clearly were its two eyes. They were two black holes of nothingness, made by the curve of four fingers and a thumb. They scanned the corridor angrily, and a hole of a mouth gave another roar as the empty eyes impossibly saw them.

'Come on,' shouted Martha, and pulled Monro a little faster.

The monster gave chase once more.

Alexander Monro ran, forcing his feet to fall in a steady rhythm lest he lose his step and fall to the ground to wait to die. The girl Martha was running behind him. She was younger and fitter, and he knew that she would have gone faster but for him. He was leading the way, out of the Surgeon's Hall courtyard and up onto the main road. He hoped that once they were back onto the High Street, she would know the way to the Castle and her friend: if he had to be the one to lead them, then the creature at their heels would have them for certain.

Alexander.

The creature was no creature. It was him, but for the grace of providence. He should not think of it as inhuman. He should not be afraid of it. He should not run from it, but turn and embrace what he had become. And yet he kept on running, leading Martha behind him. He told himself that she needed leading, before he could do what he should.

'Move! Run!' Martha shouted as they ran. 'Get out the way!'

The people on the street ignored her, or at the very most glanced her way and tutted to themselves. As

Alexander appeared behind them, however, they soon took heed. Poor Alexander: his flesh was completely obscured by the grey hands now, and they had taken on a rudimentary human form. Was he still under there, buried? Or had they simply used him as the template for their design and then subsumed him? He ran as fast as he could in pursuit of them, but his size and the panic of the people he barged heedlessly through slowed him down as much as Monro's age slowed him.

But Monro knew which of them could keep up this pace the longest.

'Ah!' Martha called suddenly. 'I know this bit. Come on!'

And she turned suddenly, leading them up the slope of the so-called Royal Mile. Monro found himself behind her again, being dragged as much as he was running up the street. Climbing the hill fast took its toll, however, and his breaths became more ragged, sharper. He felt a little stab with each inhalation, and a stitch was growing in his right-hand side. He knew with cold certainty that he couldn't make the brow of the hill.

He stopped and panted.

Alexander wasn't behind them, but the screams grew louder.

He would not be far away.

They ran on, but Monro knew it would only be a matter of time. Martha could escape without him slowing her down, he had no doubt, but he also knew that she would not leave him. He would be the cause of her capture twice over, first by slowing her down and once again because it was himself that was pursuing them. It was an impossible situation: the only thing he could think was to force her to throw down the hand that she held and let it scamper back to join Alexander, but in his present state he could barely force the breath into his body, let alone force a young girl in the prime of her life to do what she didn't wish to.

The Royal Exchange was looming up on their right.

He had an idea.

'This way,' he called to Martha.

She looked over her shoulder, but didn't seem inclined to follow him. He didn't leave her much choice, and hurried over to the Exchange's stone pillars. Between them, he could see the courtyard and the dark arches of the actual exchange beyond it, but it was not the building he was aiming for. He glanced in Martha's direction, and was pleased to see that after a moment of indecision she had opted to follow him. He had been right that she wouldn't leave him, then.

The arch of Warriston's Close appeared on their

right, and Monro hobbled down it, Martha close behind him. They both heard the screams and shouts from the street take a louder pitch: Alexander had made it onto the High Street. Monro only hoped that he had not seen where they had gone, and they could lose him for long enough to regain their breath. He pushed on through Writer's Court and the dusty, closed doorway waiting there. If it was locked, then all was lost.

'In there?' Martha asked. 'We can't hide in a building. We'll be trapped.'

Monro ignored her and tried the door. It complained loudly, but it swung open. Fortune was with them. A long flight of stairs descending into darkness was revealed, and Monro motioned for Martha to take them. She looked at him uncertainly, and wasted precious time.

'Mary King's Close,' Monro repeated, ushering her inside. 'It was sealed at this end when they built the Royal Exchange over it, but it is still open at the Nor' Loch end. If we hurry, Alexander will not think to follow, and we can follow the Loch to the Castle at our own pace. Please. If he sees us descend, he will follow.'

Martha looked over her shoulder nervously.

'You're sure Alexander won't think of it?' she asked. 'He is you, you know.'

'Martha, please!'

And so she descended.

Martha kept her hand against the wall as she walked unsteadily down the rough steps: one false move, and she would be going head over heels, and the staircase was so dark that she had no idea how far it was to the bottom. In fact, she had no idea how far it was to the next step. All she could do was place one foot carefully after the next, and listen to the rasping of Monro's breath behind her.

She hoped he had shut the door behind them.

'Keep going,' Monro encouraged behind her. 'It is not far.'

Martha stumbled as she hit the last step and tried to move down to the next, and she almost found the ground with her face. Monro put out his arms and caught her, but she had already steadied herself. She gave him a smile of thanks, and then took a glance around her. They were in a small alleyway with a dusty dirt floor that led away from the stairs and into the gloom. If this was Mary King's Close, then they were going to die here.

'This is just the entranceway,' Monro assured her, reading her mind. 'The Close is further in, and there will be places to hide and catch our breath. Move down a little way, and you'll see.'

Martha did as she was told, and found that the alleyway did bend round to the left. As she reached the turning, she could look down and see the Close spread out before her.

It ran down the side of the hill, the same dirt floor dropping away alarmingly fast as it went down to the Loch below: she wondered how many people had tripped at the top and found themselves suddenly at the bottom before they'd sealed it off. Looking up, the sky was blocked by rough wooden slats that she could only assume were the foundations of the Royal Exchange above her. Martha had seen some pretty strange things on her travels with the Doctor, but somehow the idea of an underground street somewhere as close to home as Edinburgh was almost as unsettling.

'I don't suppose they left us any lights down here, did they?' Martha asked, looking around.

'There may be some gas lamps in one of the turnpike houses,' Monro suggested. 'The merchants were required to put them out on the streets. Even before they built the exchange above us, it was usually this dark down here.'

'Really?' Martha asked.

'The houses go so far up,' Monro explained, 'they block out most of the light. And then when the washing is hung between the houses…'

Martha took a few steps down the Close and looked up, and realised what he meant: as the road sloped quickly away, the houses all remained on the same level, extra storeys appearing every few steps. The houses seemed to be much lower than she would have expected, and the only way to get up to the higher rooms was by a rickety spiral staircase that ran up the outside of the building. Martha couldn't imagine what you did if you lived in the top house and met someone going in the opposite direction when you were halfway up.

The disembodied hand twitched uncomfortably in her grasp.

'Was that why they closed them off?' Martha asked.

'I don't understand,' Monro said.

She looked around her.

'People couldn't live here,' she said.

'They still do by the Lochside,' Monro answered. He pointed down to where the gloom seemed to lighten just a little a few yards down the slope. 'All the Closes are the same. We wouldn't have the room without the turnpike houses.'

Martha looked again at the low little houses, piled up on top of each other and crumbling so badly they looked like they wouldn't last another few weeks. There was a foul smell in the air, which she was almost certain was the Loch at the bottom of the slope. She couldn't imagine anyone living here of their own free will: it was worse than the worst London had to offer, and that was bad enough.

She heard a noise behind them.

'The houses are empty,' Monro whispered, his eyes wide. 'We should be able to get through to the next Close. We can rest there.'

Martha nodded, and let Monro lead the way. She held her free hand out to him, and was glad that he had taken it the moment he led them inside the first house. She had to duck to avoid knocking her head on the ceiling, and without lights or lamps the room was in almost pitch darkness. For a moment, she nearly dropped the struggling hand she was holding to reach out for the light switch. Then she remembered.

'This way,' Monro hissed in her ear.

She couldn't see which way he was heading, but felt his hand pull her gently into the darkness. She couldn't even see the faint shape of his back in front of her any more, and she could feel her heart starting to flutter. If he meant her any harm, if perhaps he felt closer to the hands and Alexander than he did to the rest of the human race, she couldn't have picked a better place to follow him where she would never be heard of again.

She took a deep breath and told herself to think

about something else. Monro was on her side, and he was just as frightened of the hands as she was. And if he wasn't… well, she'd just have to wait for him to show some sign of it before she worried about it.

The darkness was so thick, she thought she could feel it brushing her skin. Either that, or they were walking through cobwebs. There was a faint scuttling sound coming from somewhere behind them. Martha began to wish that everything she'd been told about carrots as a child was right. She tried blinking, but still all she could see was soupy, impenetrable blackness.

'Mr Monro?' she whispered.

He shushed her quietly, but gently squeezed her hand.

Martha was starting to realise that she really didn't like the dark.

Suddenly, the hand creature she was clutching so tightly gave a jolt and began struggling like crazy. Even though she knew what it was, Martha couldn't help but react with panic. The creature had tricked her into thinking it had gone to sleep, it had been so still and gentle: now it was going crazy, digging its nails into her flesh to escape. Martha had to use both hands to try and keep hold, but even that was no good. She felt a sharp pain across the back of her hand and cried out, standing upright and banging her head against the ceiling again. Her hands came together automatically, trying to stop the blood that was barely flowing.

She dropped the hand and heard it scuttle away on the dry floor.

'Great!' she hissed.

For a moment, she considered giving chase, but it was hopeless: all she would do was stumble around in the darkness without even knowing if it was making rude gestures just inches from her face. Even if she could follow it, she knew exactly where it would be heading: she didn't want to stumble into Alexander in these dark little rooms. It was a fairly safe bet that the hand would be back soon anyway, leading that grey giant behind it. She'd much rather she wasn't here alone when it arrived. She had to get to the Doctor.

That was when Martha realised.

'Mr Monro?' she whispered, waiting for his answering shush.

She couldn't hear anything, just the sound of fingers drumming against dusty streets and rotting wooden floorboard. She took a small step forwards, squinting and holding her hands out in front of her. With every movement, she hoped to feel the cloth of Monro's jacket against her fingertips. Or the cold clamminess of Alexander's grey skin.

'Mr Monro?' she risked raising her voice a little.

Still no answer. She was alone.

'Oh no,' she said softly.

There was a part of Martha that wanted to curl up in a ball on the floor and close her eyes against the darkness, despite the rest of her knowing that staying put would only make it all the easier for the hand to find her. She couldn't see a thing anyway. And where would she go? Perhaps if she waited here, Monro would find her again and lead her to safety.

Something scuttled across the floorboards above her head.

No amount of triple-sun sunsets could be worth this.

Martha closed her eyes and dug into her pocket. The mobile phone's screen lit up as she turned it on, and she waved it in front of her. The light it gave out wasn't much to write home about, but it might stop her walking straight into a wall. She took a small step forwards, stopped and let out a breath. OK. Then she took another step.

Suddenly, the phone went dead.

Martha's heart skipped in her chest, until she realised that the display had just timed out. She hit a button at random, and the pale green light returned. She let out another breath, and stepped slowly forward. With every inch she moved, she kept expecting to touch some cold, dank, unspeakable horror that would just make her scream and run away. But she didn't. The sound of the scuttling was growing louder, sounding like someone drumming in the street outside. She took a step forwards.

The light from the phone made a small green square on the wall.

Waving the phone around and pressing buttons at random, Martha quickly managed to follow the wall until the light vanished into a black hole. Trying not to give a shout of triumph, Martha quickly felt all around the gap: it was a doorway! A low, open doorway! She hurried through it as fast as she dared in the darkness.

For a moment, she wondered if she had even left the room she had been standing in. The drumming of racing fingertips was still just as loud, and the room was still just as dark.

She was about to whisper for Monro again, when she saw something at the far end of the room. Nothing definite, just the vague sensation of something reflecting the pale green light of her mobile. The gentle dancing of motes in daylight.

Martha hurried over, the light getting less faint with each step so that by the time she was at the far side of the room she felt comfortable enough to move without holding her hands out in front of her face. It was a wonderful feeling, having even such a faint and greasy light come back to her: if it was up to her, she would spend the rest of her life above ground and in the sunshine.

Somewhere, somebody screamed.

Martha's heart jumped again.

'Mr Monro?' she called, not even thinking to whisper. 'Mr Monro?'

There was a sound behind her, something moving in the darkness she had just left. Martha spun around, and, for just a moment, there was something there. Like the vague afterimage of a candle on the eye once you'd blown it out, she could see a shape at the far end of the room. The room suddenly felt icy cold, and there was an overpowering smell of oiled leather everywhere.

The thing at the end of the room was a man.

It was there for just a moment, a man covered head to toe in a long black leather coat and a broad-brimmed hat. Martha was so surprised to see him there that she took a step towards him, about to call to him. He saw her first, and turned into the light. His face wasn't a human face: instead, he had the long curved beak of a raven and peered at her with two glistening black eyes.

FIFTEEN

By the time McAllister and the Doctor reached the raft, the two hand creatures had already dived into the Loch and were halfway to the other side. They seemed to have taken the vague form of two giant dogs, both about the size of a St Bernard. The Doctor could only begin to imagine what particular quirk of DNA had caused that, unless the shape had been consciously chosen for the advantage it would give it on land and in water. Which would suggest intelligence.

'Don't take your eyes off those hands,' the Doctor shouted to McAllister as they pushed the raft back into the water. 'If we lose them, that's it.'

McAllister scowled at the Doctor, but saved his breath.

The Doctor grabbed an oar and started to paddle furiously, but the two creatures were very nearly at the other side of the Loch before he even managed to get a good rhythm up. McAllister uttered a small string of curses under his breath, and helped with the rowing whilst keeping the hands clearly in sight. They still weren't going to be fast enough, even with the both of them. What the Doctor wouldn't have given for a good anachronistic outboard motor.

Instead, he had to settle for a stroke of luck.

As the two doggy creatures reached the other side of the Loch, they pulled themselves up onto the shore and looked, just for a moment, as if they might start shaking their fur dry. Instead, their front legs briefly brushed against each other – but where they came together, they didn't come apart again. McAllister's mouth fell open as the two dogs opened up into two balls of waggling fingers that started very deliberately to interlock into one shape.

'Don't stop paddling!' the Doctor shouted.

They managed to get the raft nearly three-quarters of the way across the Loch before the two creatures lifted themselves back up again. Except that now they were one: a large stocky man-mountain with trunk-like legs and broad shoulders. The man-thing gave a quick look over one shoulder at the approaching raft, and then started jogging along the edge of the Loch.

The Doctor dropped his paddle and stood up on the raft, watching for just a moment.

It was a shame. It was always difficult to get the TARDIS to land near a good dry cleaners. And he really was fond of his blue suit.

'Row!' McAllister shouted.

The Doctor dived into the Loch.

The water was cold, and shot into his ears, nose and mouth. It tasted foul but, as he came up, he powered himself forward through the water, wishing he'd thought to take off his heavy coat. The Doctor heard the sound of McAllister diving inexpertly into the water behind him. Why did nobody ever listen when he told them what to do?

The Doctor reached the shore, looking up quickly enough to see the creature loping away towards the town. Behind him, McAllister was struggling in the water, unwilling to open his eyes and see where he was in case the slime got into them. The Doctor tutted impatiently and waded in to pull him out. The soldier coughed brackish water as he struggled to his feet, and then looked around for the creature.

'It went this way,' the Doctor said. 'If we hurry, we might catch it.'

McAllister gave him a shrewd look.

'I may have misjudged you, Doctor,' he said flatly. 'You're a brave man.'

The Doctor smiled and smoothed down his wet hair.

'If anything you do harms this town,' McAllister continued, 'I'll see you strung up in the Grassmarket and your head on a spike on the Castle walls.'

The Doctor nodded. 'A traditionalist, then,' he said.

And then they ran.

The grassy slope of Castle Hill was starting to give way to large ramshackle wooden buildings and narrow streets that ran steeply up to the Royal Mile. Even down here, there were plenty of people about, and the way they were either shouting, hiding or crying suggested that their hand-man had come this way. There was a man clutching onto a tired-looking donkey as if he was torn between protecting it and jumping on its back to ride to safety. His eyes were wide and his jaw had dropped: a witness if ever the Doctor had seen one. The donkey, meanwhile, was casually relieving itself into the brown waters of the Loch.

'Which way did it go?' the Doctor asked.

All the man could manage was to point down one of the narrow alleyways. McAllister nodded and hurried after it, but the Doctor hung back for just a second.

'Don't let him do that,' he said, nodding to the donkey. 'People have to swim in that.'

The Doctor didn't wait to see if the man listened to him or not. He raced away up the alley, weaving between the few people who were all trying to race in the opposite direction. The turnpike houses loomed up on either side, and the street soon got pretty gloomy. The Doctor started to remember expressions about meeting creatures at the end of dark alleys, but he put them out of his mind. In a few moments, he had caught up with McAllister. It was good to know he could still outrun someone twenty-two times younger than him.

'This is Stewart's Close,' McAllister panted. 'We'll be right under the Royal Exchange soon enough.'

The Doctor looked up: the darkness wasn't being caused by the tall houses any more, but by a rickety wooden roof overhead. Was the hand-man just running blind, or was he instinctively trying to head underground? Did he even have a plan?

'What do we do when we catch it?' McAllister asked.

From somewhere came a shout of surprise.

'Probably that,' the Doctor said. 'Come on.'

The cry had come from a little apartment just to their left, next to what seemed to be a saw-maker's workshop, still in use. The apartment had a little low door hanging open, but inside it was as black as any night the Doctor had ever known. McAllister twitched impatiently at his side, clearly thinking that if they weren't giving chase to the hand-man they were just wasting time. But the Doctor knew better than that: he had recognised the voice.

He stepped into the darkness.

'Hello Martha,' a familiar voice said from the darkness.

Martha's heart skipped, and she forgot everything except rushing over to the Doctor and squeezing him so tight she could hear the wind pushed out of his lungs. It was almost worth everything else, a moment like that. Then she felt the slime on her skin, and the smell reached her nose.

She pulled away again.

'Ugh!' she said. 'What happened to you?'

'Little swim,' the Doctor said lightly. 'What happened to you?'

Martha felt a lump appear in her throat.

'There's something in here,' she said, her voice dropping to a whisper. She tried to look around, but the misty grey light had vanished and the room was back in darkness. 'It looked like a man all dressed in leather, only he had a raven's face.'

'A beak?' the Doctor asked. He was rummaging in his pockets. 'Leather hat?'

Martha shuddered at the memory.

'That's him,' she said. 'You too?'

'I'm afraid not,' the Doctor answered. 'Sounds like you saw a plague doctor. They looked after the people who'd been struck by the pest. The leather was to protect them, and the mask was to keep the smell out. They thought the smell was the cause, you see.'

'You've brought me to a plague town?'

'This was over a hundred years ago,' the Doctor said. She felt him move away from her. 'This place has quite a reputation for ghosts. Don't worry. Doctors are the good guys.'

And suddenly, she could see him. He was standing in front of her, his arm outstretched and holding what looked like a little sun in his cupped hand. Martha nearly jumped out of her skin when she turned and saw Captain McAllister standing next to her, dripping wet and without his heavy red jacket. To her annoyance, the Captain didn't even look at her. He was looking over her shoulder.

'Of course,' the Doctor said casually, 'it might just be something else.'

The leather-clad plague doctor was standing in the corner, his raven's beak looking up at the room's other occupants: two grey giants, one of which Martha knew had once been Alexander Monro. Where the other had come from, she couldn't guess, but she clung tightly to the Doctor as it stepped forward.

The plague doctor's leathers rustled, and a solitary grey hand jumped out before melting into the giant's flesh.

The body of the doctor fell silently to the floor.

Martha bit her lip.

Pinned to the wall behind the two grey figures, the old anatomist Monro struggled. Grey disembodied hands holding his wrists and his ankles to the crumbling stonework, whilst another pair of hands clamped across his mouth, leaving only his wide and staring eyes uncovered.

Martha looked to the Doctor, but all his attention was on the grey monsters.

Suddenly they moved.

Every hand that made up the front of the two grey creatures opened its fingers wide, leaving nothing but a man-shaped mass of waggling tentacles. The two figures took a step closer to each other, and the tips of those fingers touched. They caressed, they explored and they interlocked. The hands were grasping tight to each other now, and with one sudden pull they moved so close together that it was impossible to see where the one ended and the other began.

The fingers closed in, and there was but a single creature there.

'Doctor,' Martha said, moving in protectively.

'It's all right,' the Doctor said.

Martha didn't believe him.

The creature shifted awkwardly from one foot to the other, as if testing its new legs. It was twice the size it had been before, and was cramped uncomfortably into the room. Its face was so subtly formed that every thought, every human expression passed so clearly across it; Martha couldn't believe that it was made purely from the flexing of cold fingers. Its eyes were two deep pits, and deep within each one a single fingertip flicked this way and that in mimicry of a pupil. Both eyes watched the Doctor cautiously.

'Can you talk now?' the Doctor asked.

The creature growled a little.

'That's it,' the Doctor coaxed, as if it was a stumbling child. 'Come on.'

'I…' the creature said. 'I live.'

'Yes, yes you do!' the Doctor said with a cry of triumph. He turned to Martha with a glint in his eye. 'You see that? Eh?'

Martha gave him a cold look. 'Doctor,' she said. 'Alexander's in there.'

The Doctor looked at her for a moment, and realised: the hands had been attaching themselves to the dead because they were designed to coalesce around a single body. The damage that had been done had made each individual hand try to start the process independently. When he'd repaired them, he'd inadvertently caused some poor soul to get trapped inside the creature as it formed.

'Well,' the Doctor said. 'We can't have that. Listen… have you got a name?'

The creature stood a little taller.

'I am Onk Ndell Kith,' it said proudly. 'I am alive.'

'Yes,' the Doctor agreed. 'Do you mind if I call you Kith?'

The creature looked as if it didn't have an opinion on the matter.

'So,' the Doctor said airily. 'Kith. What now?'

The creature drew itself up as much as the low ceiling would allow. In practice, this simply meant that, as it rose up, it loomed further over the Doctor. He felt McAllister shift beside him, and glanced the glint of a metal dirk hidden in his hand. This wasn't the time for heroics; the Doctor quietly twisted the knife out of the Captain's hand and dropped it into his pocket.

'I am alive,' the monster repeated, more threatening now. 'You cannot know what it has taken—'

The Doctor took offence at that.

'Oh I think I can!' he protested. 'Splitting your consciousness down into a series of self-replicating organic units? Each little one expendable on their own, so long as just one survives to clone itself again – it's brilliant! As soon as there are enough of them to reach their critical mass: boom! There you are again, right as rain.'

'You appreciate the technology,' Kith said.

'I *understand* it,' the Doctor corrected.

'I have achieved immortality,' Kith said grandly. His chest swelled with pride. 'I will never feel the touch of death.'

'And believe me, I know how hard that can be,' the Doctor said sadly. 'But that isn't quite the full story, is it?'

For a moment, Kith was silent.

'When I came here, I crashed into the water,' he answered eventually. 'My units fell into a hibernation cycle.'

'Here?' McAllister asked. 'The town?'

'The planet,' Martha answered quietly.

'This man discovered one of my units,' Kith said, pointing at where Monro was still pinned to the wall. Still staring wildly. 'He damaged it, attacking it with lightning-electricity. As it woke, it tried to use his DNA to effect a permanent repair. It did not work.'

'Doctor?' Martha said out of the corner of her mouth. 'Monro said that when he found it, the hand didn't look like a hand. Not until after it got his blood on its nails... and then it looked exactly like his.'

The Doctor nodded.

'The hand was trying to repair the damage using

Monro's DNA,' he said, fascinated. It had been a good few centuries since he'd come across a modular organism. 'It kept hold of the bits it needed from its original make-up, and replaced the rest with a clone of Monro's hand.'

'Not just his hand…' Martha said.

The Doctor's eyes widened.

'You cloned a whole person?' the Doctor said. 'Just how much damage did…'

Kith turned, letting one shoulder drop, and the Doctor's voice trailed off. In the light of his lamp, he could see a section of the creature's skin where the fingers had not joined together properly. Instead, they were swelling and turning a livid bruised colour, the nails digging uncomfortably into the swollen tissue. It didn't look natural, and it didn't look healthy.

'The imperfection remains,' Kith said softly. 'But now I am alive, I can correct it.'

'Correct it?' Martha asked, looking at the Doctor.

The Doctor didn't catch her eye.

'He needs an injection of new genetic code,' he said, before looking up at the grey giant. 'You'd have to be choosy this time though, wouldn't you? Sift through and make sure you only took the right sections. Wouldn't want to make the same mistake again. How many different samples would you need?'

The massive creature blinked.

'Eighty thousand,' it answered calmly.

'And these samples,' Martha said, standing and staring the creature in its strange eyes. 'They can just be any old DNA? If it's going to save the world, I can face a haircut.'

The Doctor shook his head.

'I'm afraid not,' he said. 'Like I said, he'd have to sift through the code very carefully. The *bad* kind of sifting.'

'You're talking about killing 80,000 people so that you don't die? That's...'

'Edinburgh,' the Doctor said coldly. 'All of it.'

There was a cold silence.

'Of course,' the Doctor said conversationally, 'the material would keep degrading. I'd give it another century or so, but I suppose there'd always be Glasgow then, wouldn't there?'

'I am alive,' Kith said.

The way he said it, the Doctor had no doubt that it was all the justification Kith needed. It was alive, and it wanted to remain so. There was no way that he could let it carry out its plan, no way in the world – it wouldn't stop until it had sifted its way through the entire human genome. Trouble was, modular organisms were depressingly hardy, so stopping Kith wasn't going to be as easy as all that.

'There is another way,' the Doctor said.

The creature sensed treachery at that, and reared up again. Its massive shoulders pushed up through the roof, sending wood, dust and rubble raining to the floor. Its hands flexed, not yet threatening anyone, but making it clear that, if it chose, there would be no mistake.

'I live,' Kith growled. There was a touch of fear in his voice now. 'I cannot die.'

The Doctor held both his hands up.

'What if I could find you some genetic coding that was special?' he asked. '*Very* special: genetic code that was constantly adapting and regenerating so that it wouldn't degrade. Well, not for another few thousand years, at any rate. You wouldn't need quite as much of that, would you? Say, about one person's worth?'

'You?' Kith asked, an eyebrow raising.

'As long as you let Alexander and anyone else you've got floating around in there go,' the Doctor said. 'Me.'

'No!' Martha said, pulling at the Doctor's arm. 'You can't do that. Let me. Take me instead.'

The Doctor shook his head sadly.

'Time Lord DNA,' he said.

Tears were starting to prick the corners of Martha's eyes. They glistened in the burning lamplight.

'Look, there'll probably be something left of me when Kith's finished,' the Doctor said with careful cheerfulness. 'I need you to do something for me. Martha?'

'What?' she asked quietly.

'Take me to the TARDIS,' he said, looking imploringly into her eyes. 'Tell it you're activating the Laika Protocol. She'll tell you what to do next.'

'A hologram?' Martha asked.

'Yes, a…' the Doctor paused for a second.

'What?'

'Doesn't matter.'

'Doctor?'

'Nothing,' the Doctor said, waving his hand. Martha fixed him with a glare. 'Just… well, just don't take it the wrong way if it calls you Rose.'

Martha's glare deepened and, for just a moment, the Doctor thought he needn't worry about Kith killing him.

The Doctor gave Martha a hug, and whispered in her ear. She nodded quietly and stepped back, her tears drying. He gave her a smile, and she tried to return it. Neither of them said goodbye. The Doctor gave a quick salute to McAllister, which he returned sharply, and then the Doctor turned back to the grey giant that stood silently watching them.

He held out his hand to the creature.

'Well?' he said. 'Take my hand?'

SIXTEEN

It was a strange feeling, all in all, and one that the Doctor could probably have missed out on quite happily. Kith's flesh was cold to the touch, even for him, and, as soon as one hand had grasped the Doctor's, others began to detach themselves from the hand-man's body and crawl over him. The Doctor dropped his lamp, and it rolled to the corner of the room, throwing strange shadows across the walls until the hands closed over his eyes. The last thing he saw was Martha.

She'd get over losing him. Eventually.

As the hands closed over his flesh, he felt that strange disassociation that he always felt whenever he had other people over to stay in his head. The uncomfortable feeling of another intelligence barging you out of the way and slowly taking control of all the bits you never thought about being in control of until you weren't. He could feel Kith taking stock of his new possession – or was it possessee? – and sifting through every bit of it, inch by inch.

The Doctor could feel the hands around him starting to draw out little pieces of his biodata, turning them over and pulling them apart to see how they worked. To see what they could use. By the time they had finished, the little creatures would have taken the best of him: he would be nothing, and they would be running around regenerating to their little hearts' content. It was ironic. Here he was, the last of the Time Lords, but when he was dead there would be practically thousands of them again. It was almost satisfying.

He winced as the hands started to dig deep.

Kith had reached his memories, and was carefully dredging through them all, even the ugly ones. There were things there that even the Doctor didn't want to see again, but Kith was nothing if not thorough. He was going to find the use of every last strand of DNA, RNA and any other three-letter acronyms he might come across.

Dying to save Edinburgh, the Doctor thought. It could be worse.

Suddenly, the Doctor felt the hands that covered

him twitch as one, and something related to both light and pain flashed across his brain. This was it, after all this time. Time to say goodbye. He felt all the heat leech from his body, and could smell a musty scent all around him. There was a light burning in the distance, and he tried to head for it, but he remained stubbornly where he was.

A moment passed.

'Doctor?' asked a voice, light and feminine.

This was it.

'Doctor?' echoed another voice. Deeper and gruffer.

Was he hallucinating, or was that...

The Doctor opened his eyes, and was nearly blinded by his own lamp burning just inches away from his face. As he recoiled, the lamp was pulled away and three blurry red shapes resolved themselves into the faces of Martha, McAllister and Monro. The Doctor blinked up at them for a moment, and then turned his head. He was lying on his back on the cold dusty floor. There was no sign of Kith anywhere about.

'What happened?' he asked, his voice cracking.

'Careful!' Martha warned, still the doctor, even with him.

He ignored her. He was, after all, *the* Doctor.

'What happened?' he asked again, pulling himself upright. 'Where's Kith?'

'I don't know,' Martha said. She glanced to McAllister. 'He was all over you – it looked like he was going to smother you – and then… Then he just stopped and let you go. He ran off back up the street and left you lying there. How do you feel?'

'No no,' the Doctor complained. He realised that the musty smell was his own damp clothes; he really needed to find a dry cleaner. 'He wouldn't just go. His genetic structure's unravelling – he'll be dead inside a week. He needed my DNA to repair himself.'

'And he doesn't have it?' Monro asked.

The Doctor tried to make allowances for the fact that this was a good hundred years before the discovery of 'nuclein'.

'No,' he said. 'He doesn't.'

'Then clearly he doesn't need it,' McAllister said.

'But he does!' the Doctor protested. 'If he… unless…'

Oh no.

'Unless he found out about a better option!'

The TARDIS!

Monro rubbed his sore wrists to try and get the blood pumping back into them, and only then looked to his rescuers. They hadn't needed to go far to find which way Alexander had gone: the walls of the houses nearest to them were crumbling, stones and dust raining down on them. He had clearly taken the shortest route back to the High Street, climbing straight up the sides of the buildings and across the rooftops. The sound of the screaming had reached them even down in the darkness of the Close. Monro looked to Martha and the stranger, and wondered when his life had become this confusing nightmare.

'We have to follow,' the guardsman said. 'If we lose it—'

'It's heading for the Castle,' the stranger said grimly.

'How do you know?'

'Because that's where the TARDIS is,' he answered.

Martha looked shocked.

'The TARDIS?'

'Which would you rather be?' the stranger asked her. 'A Time Lord stuck on a primitive world for the next thousand years, or his living time ship with the whole universe to explore?'

Monro hoped it wasn't a question he was going to be asked.

'What are we going to do?' Martha asked.

The stranger was reaching into his dripping coat. He pulled out a short metal tube with a glowing end. His fingers danced across it for a moment, and the blue light glowed a little deeper. It caught his face, lighting it from below and giving him a ghastly pallor. His face was full of grim anger, and Monro knew that there was nothing that he wouldn't do to stop Alexander, himself, his son. He felt afraid, and wondered if this was how others had felt as they'd seen the corpses walking.

'I might be able to disrupt the electric field that holds the hands together,' the stranger was saying. 'I haven't got the power to do any permanent damage, but it will hurt.'

Monro looked at him.

'Hurt?' he said. 'Hurt Alexander?'

'Alexander?' the stranger asked.

Martha stepped forward and put a hand on the stranger's arm.

'Alexander's his…' She trailed off. 'It's complicated. But he's inside that creature.'

The stranger fixed Monro with steely eyes.

'I'm so sorry,' he said.

The screams grew louder, and they all looked up. They wouldn't wait any longer: they would give chase, and they would hurt Alexander. Monro remembered holding him as a babe, the way he had looked up at him knowingly and squeezed his finger so tight. It was strange, because he knew that inside his head, Alexander was him. Perfectly him. But he had also been a child, and Monro had been his father. And the stranger would kill him if it would save his 'TARDIS'.

Monro jumped forward and snatched the tube from the stranger's hand.

'Hey!' the stranger shouted, but Monro was already gone.

He ran down the slope of the Close so fast that he feared his feet might overtake him and he would end up falling, but by some good grace he kept going. The tube felt hot in its hand, perhaps angry that it had been taken from its master. He had to keep it from him, to protect Alexander. He had to find him, and protect him. Or join him.

He glanced over his shoulder.

Martha was giving chase.

McAllister pulled the Doctor with him as they raced up the rickety stairs to the High Street: they were both starting to tire, so perhaps it took them longer than it should have done. It would be good to finally lie down at the end of all this, even if it was to be in death. The Doctor had struggled for a brief moment, wanting to join the girl in chasing down Monro, but McAllister wouldn't allow it: the Doctor was perhaps the only one who knew exactly what this enemy was, and if he was going to protect the Castle from it, McAllister could only do it with his help.

'You can stop it?' McAllister panted as they ran.

'I don't know,' the Doctor admitted.

They burst out of the Close and back onto the High Street, where people were either running as fast as they could away from the Castle, or else lying insensible in the street. McAllister didn't want to guess how many of them might never get up again. Even one would be too many. Looking up the street, more people were racing towards them in panic. Bouncing across the rooftops, scattering tiles and stonework to the ground in a deadly shower, the massive grey shape of the creature moved.

'Sir,' came a crisp voice across the chaos.

McAllister spun. A young soldier in a dirty red coat saluted.

'William Marsden Howkins,' he announced. 'Reporting for duty.'

McAllister found himself smiling, just for a moment.

'You evacuated the church?' he asked. 'Were there any losses?'

'None, sir,' Howkins answered. 'We regrouped at the Tolbooth, awaiting orders.'

McAllister nodded, and then turned his head sharply as a terrible thunder came from further down the road. One of the buildings that the creature was dancing across wasn't as strong as the others, and the whole roof had given way as soon as its feet had landed. There was a shower of wood and stone and slate, and in the middle of it was the creature, suddenly spinning without footing. All of it landed with a loud crash onto the cobbles below.

McAllister prayed that the street and the houses had been empty.

Then he looked to the Doctor.

'Nothing I say will stop you,' he said to the Captain grimly. 'But your men would do better to get the townsfolk to safety. You're not going to do it any harm with muskets and cannons.'

McAllister nodded briskly, and spun.

'Gather the men, Howkins,' he barked. 'And none of your sloppiness: I want to see rank and file here before I count to ten. Any soldier not here and carrying his musket will be considered a coward and a deserter, am I understood? Now MOVE!'

McAllister spun back to the Doctor, but he had already gone.

God help them all.

Monro might have been an old man, but he could move when he had to: he kept ahead of Martha all the way down to the Loch and then along it, circling back to the Castle. It was only as he started the steep climb back up to the stone walls that Martha even managed to get near him. She didn't know what she was going to do when she caught up. Make him see reason, somehow. Even though she knew there was no way in the world her father would see reason if somebody threatened to hurt her.

Then she looked up, and saw there was no chance.

Monro was still a good few yards ahead of her, and he was shouting up at the Castle walls, throwing his hands out in supplication. But he wasn't appealing to God. He was calling to the massive creature that was clinging to the side of the Castle, pulling itself up inch by inch without even a glance behind it. A couple of red-coated soldiers were standing on the walls, firing their muskets down at the creature, but it was having no impact at all. Martha shouted at them to run, but they couldn't hear her.

Martha recognised the spot as pretty close to where they had parked the TARDIS. Kith was going to make it to the time machine before she even had a chance of catching Monro.

The two soldiers disappeared briefly from the wall, before returning hefting a large pot between them. Martha's first thought was that they were going to pour boiling oil over Kith, but instead it was the pot itself that was thrown over the ramparts, striking the creature a glancing blow as it fell. Kith barely even noticed it but, as Martha ran, she saw four hands detach themselves from his body and scuttle at speed up the wall. She had to turn away for a second to jump out of the way of the pot that was rolling down the hill towards her. When she looked up again there was no sign of the hands or the soldiers.

Kith just kept climbing.

Monro reached the foot of the walls, and looked for a moment as if he might try to follow the creature up. But he was old, and he was tired, and Martha doubted that he had ever been rock climbing in his life: instead, he jumped up and down at the bottom of the wall and shouted up to try to attract the attention of his 'son'. Martha was close enough now that she could hear what he was shouting.

'Alexander!' Monro yelled, jumping around like the ground was on fire. 'Please! Don't leave me here to die! Take me with you: make me like you! Anything. Just please don't leave me!'

Martha wouldn't have thought that there was anything of Alexander left inside the creature, so she was surprised when it stopped climbing for a moment and looked down over its shoulder.

'Please!' Monro pleaded, quietly.

Kith held out a hand towards the anatomist, as if he was going to reach down and pluck him up to safety. Monro held both his hands high, straining to reach, but Kith was still too high up the wall for the two to touch. Instead, Kith's hand twitched and one of the little grey disembodied hands that made it up detached itself and fell to the ground. As Kith turned back and continued his climb up the wall, the disembodied hand fell onto Monro and started to throttle him.

As Martha reached Monro, he was already turning blue. His eyes were wide and staring, panic already well in control of him. He had his hands at his neck trying to pull the grey hand away, but it had dug in so tightly that its sharp nails were already sending a steady trickle of blood down the old man's neck. Martha quickly looked around her on the ground. There!

'Don't worry,' she told Monro.

She scooped the sonic screwdriver up from where Monro had dropped it and turned it on.

The effect as she pointed it at the grey hand was startling: it starting to twitch and buck, losing control over its own fingers and eventually dropping from Monro's neck. The anatomist sat on the floor, gasping for breath and clutching at his neck. The hand kept twitching on the ground. As soon as Martha turned the sonic screwdriver away from it, however, it righted itself, looking as if it might attack again. The Doctor hadn't been kidding when he said that the screwdriver wouldn't do any permanent harm.

Martha turned the screwdriver back on the hand and, whilst it twitched at her feet, she gave it a good sharp kick. It flew into the air and landed on the ground a good few feet away, bouncing down the hill until it landed with a plop in the waters of the Nor' Loch. Martha didn't even wait to see if it started swimming out again. She gave Monro a quick look to see he was still breathing, and then stepped up to the Castle wall.

She pointed the screwdriver up at Kith and turned it on.

The effect was instant.

The hands that had joined to make Kith's new body all began to twitch as the screwdriver pointed at them, shaking so much that they lost their hold on each other and started raining down onto Martha. But as soon as they were out of the line of fire, they regained their senses and started to attack. She was getting covered in the little creatures, but still she stood and struggled to point the wand upwards.

The hands were vicious and furious, sharp little nails clawing into every inch of exposed skin. She screwed her eyes shut and tried to shake them from her face, all the while keeping the screwdriver pointed up into the air. She didn't even know if she was still aiming at Kith. All she knew was that the Doctor needed her to do this, and she would do it. Even if it was the death of her.

'Martha!' came a shout from above.

She recognised the voice and opened her eyes.

The Doctor was there, leaning over the Castle walls. How he'd managed to get to the Castle before them, she couldn't imagine, but it was enough to make her spirits rise, even as the murderous hands continued to rain down on her. In his hand, the Doctor was clutching the red, white and blue livery of the Union Flag: he must have plucked if from a flagpole somewhere around the Castle.

'Turn it off!' he shouted down. 'Turn it off!'

Martha hesitated only for a moment before letting the sonic screwdriver die, and then she was struggling and shaking the grey hands from her. With the screwdriver disabled, they didn't seem interested in attacking her any longer. Most of the hands were climbing back up the wall to rejoin the rest of Kith's flesh.

Kith resumed his climb up the Castle wall.

'Doctor!' Martha shouted.

But he had vanished from sight.

The Doctor stood and caught his breath while he waited. Kith would be there soon, and then he would find out whether his plan was suicidal, or just dangerously foolish. The flag he held tugged in the breeze, and he looked up briefly at the grey skies above. Standing around in wet clothes and a cold wind was starting to take the spring out of even his step. In his pocket, he fingered the end of the reel of wire. He'd only just had time to snatch it from the TARDIS and get back outside, the freezing wind making his fingers thick and numb as they tried to tie the knots.

Two massive grey hands appeared over the side of the wall.

Kith pulled himself over and onto the ramparts. Like the city it protected, the Castle was built on several layers and, whilst the other side of the wall was a sheer drop, on the inside it was only a few feet down to the ground. St Margaret's Chapel was behind them, but the hand-man wasn't interested in that. He was interested in the large blue box that was resting on the walkway, hidden from prying eyes by the chapel's historic brickwork.

Kith growled, and flexed his hand-made muscles.

'No sonic devices,' the Doctor said, taking a step forward to show that all he held was the Union Flag. 'Just talk. All right?'

Kith took a step closer, pulling himself up to his full height. He was nearly half as tall again as the Doctor and, if he wanted, those massive hands could probably snap the Time Lord in two without much trouble. The Doctor stepped forward again, keeping himself firmly in the hand-man's path to the TARDIS.

'No more talk,' Kith said.

The Doctor held up his hands.

'You don't want to do this,' he said earnestly. 'She's the last TARDIS in the whole universe. You have no idea what she might do to protect herself.'

'*You* have no idea what *I* will do,' Kith countered.

'You just want to live,' the Doctor said. 'I can understand that. Believe me.'

'Then move, or I will kill you.'

'Take me,' the Doctor said again. He was close enough now to reach out and touch Kith's cold grey skin, but he didn't. He just stared imploringly into his empty eyes. 'You can use my DNA and repair yourself – regenerate instead of just falling apart again. Nobody will try and stop you, I'll make sure of that. Just leave the TARDIS alone.'

For just a moment, the Doctor thought he might agree.

'You are remarkable,' Kith said. 'But she is immortal.'

The Doctor saw a handful of redcoats rushing into the courtyard below, each taking a position to cover Kith with a musket and waiting for McAllister to give the order. Martha and Monro were with them, further back, with Martha giving the older man an examination before helping him to rest against a wall. Kith saw them too, and pushed gruffly past the Doctor as if he wasn't there, as he could have done at any time.

'Hold on, Alexander,' the Doctor said as he fell to the floor.

He rolled quickly and was on his feet again.

'Hold your fire!' he shouted to McAllister.

He didn't think it would work, but somehow he seemed to have earned the Captain's trust. McAllister didn't give the order, even as Kith paced steadily towards the TARDIS. The Doctor took the flag in his hands and twisted it, the sticks that he had inserted into it locking together into a taut frame. The TARDIS key bounced against the kite's spine, tied there by a length of the thin metal wire. Kith didn't even glance back, and the Doctor couldn't wait: he mentally crossed his fingers and launched the kite into the air.

The cold Edinburgh wind took it, and suddenly it soared upwards into the clouds, spinning a couple of times before disappearing into the grey. But it wasn't lost for ever: that thin metal filament stretched down out of the sky, pulling tighter with every second that passed. But it wasn't the Doctor holding onto the kite-string. Kith took another step forward and felt something tug, and as he looked down at his own leg, he saw one of the hands that made it up was clinging tightly onto the metal string. He looked up at the Doctor with a look of surprise on his face.

'Keep holding on, Alexander,' the Doctor said.

The thing that most people didn't understand, the

Doctor thought in the second he had, was that it didn't have to be the middle of a raging storm. They thought that the kite had gone up and the lightning had struck it, running down the string to the ground. But that wasn't it. If it had been, anyone holding the string would have been fried in an instant. No, the beauty of it was the key: the key was tied to the kite and went up into the clouds, and up there it soaked up the electricity waiting in the storm clouds without it ever earthing down the string. Once the kite was pulled down, the electricity in the key could be transferred to a chemical battery, and used to prove that lightning and earthly electricity were one and the same.

Of course, Franklin probably wouldn't be very happy with the Doctor's version of it: he had tied the key directly to the kite-string, and that was just plain dangerous. For whoever was holding the string. The TARDIS key did its work, sucking the electricity out of the clouds and subtly changing it before sending it racing to the ground below. There was a flash of sparks and an angry boom, and Kith let out a monstrous roar. The Doctor stood for a moment, watching the electricity playing all over his body.

'I'm sorry. I'm so sorry,' he said. Then he turned and shouted: 'Martha! Use the screwdriver!'

Martha ran forward from the courtyard below and held the sonic screwdriver aloft. The Doctor winced as its ultrasonic wail made his ears ache, but the effect was even more dramatic on Kith. He roared again, and each of the individual hands that made up his body seemed to throw their fingers up and quiver. He staggered this way and that, before hitting the low wall that separated him from the long drop below.

The Doctor dashed forwards and grabbed at the hand holding onto the kite-string. He winced as he touched it. Most of the electricity had already earthed into Kith, but enough still remained to be uncomfortable. He gave the hand a sharp tug and prayed that he'd tied the knot at the top correctly. As he held tight to the hand, his fingers screaming at the current flowing through them, the rest of Kith's body toppled in slow motion over the edge of the Castle walls. Kith fell away in a shower of unmoving grey hands, and Alexander Monro appeared from the mess to fall to the floor.

The Doctor spared a quick look over the ramparts, seeing the smoking hands falling apart as they bounced down into the murky waters of the Loch. From somewhere behind him, there was a quiet tinkle and the Doctor spun around to see the TARDIS key lying on the stonework, the metal string still tightly wrapped around it.

He'd tied the knot right after all.

***

Alexander could barely feel the cold stones at his back, could only feel the fire in his lungs and in his hand. He had vague, smoky memories of what had happened and why he was here, but as he tried to reach for them they blew between his fingers and drifted away. All he could feel with any clarity was that electric dread in the pit of his stomach that told him he was dying.

He blinked tears from his eyes, and saw a stranger standing over him.

'Hello,' he said. 'I'm the Doctor.'

A doctor. So he *was* dying.

'It isn't fair,' he croaked pitifully. 'I just needed more time. There is so much left that I haven't done!'

'I know,' the Doctor said gently. 'You're right: it isn't fair. Life is too short, and there's always something else you missed. It isn't right, and it isn't fair. But it is how it is, and there's no escaping it. Life is precious, and it's short. Everything has its time.'

As he said it, Alexander could feel his sadness.

Then the Doctor's eyes turned to steel as he looked down.

'But how can you enjoy the ride,' he said, sternly, 'if you're always worrying when it will be over?'

Alexander felt his consciousness slipping away, perhaps for the last time. As it went, he considered the Doctor's words. What kind of a life had he had? He had made advancements, medical techniques that might live on after him, but what else? A fear that had always been with him, sapping him and making him a frightened child again in the night. A life spent trying to find a way, any way, to prevent the inevitable, and only when it had finally found him did he realise that that was no life at all.

'It's all right,' the Doctor was saying to somebody. 'It's just Alexander Monro. He's a lecturer at the university. Like his father before him.'

'Is he dead?' asked a brisk soldier's voice.

A pause then.

'No,' the Doctor said softly. 'It's not his time.'

EDINBURGH, 1997

SEVENTEEN

It was a beautiful bright day, the sky a fantastic shade of blue that made Martha think of picnics and beer gardens. Instead, they were standing at the top of what the Doctor informed her was called Calton Hill, in the centre of a triangle that was made by the row of Greek-looking columns, a Roman-looking monument and something that could easily have been a lighthouse. They were anything but alone up here: the Festival was in full swing, and the city was at its busiest. The Doctor had promised that he'd take her to see a good production of *Measure for Measure* later on, but for now he was just watching over the city with a huge grin on his face.

'Isn't it marvellous?' he said with a grin.

Martha looked out at the view. Most of what she

could see hadn't even been built the last time she was here, the New Town sprawling out away from the Old and racing down towards the Firth of Forth. The houses looked grand and the streets wide, but Martha couldn't quite forget the narrow rooms with the low ceilings that the people in the Old Town had been forced to live in, crammed on top of each other like makeshift tower blocks.

'They're still there,' the Doctor said, doing his mind-reading act. 'The Closes: underneath the Royal Exchange. Well, the City Chambers now: they say the merchants didn't want to leave the streets, but I think they were more worried another monster was going to come running out.'

Martha gave a little shudder. If she spoke to anybody here about it, it would just be ancient history to them.

But to her it was yesterday.

'What about the Loch?' she asked. 'What happened to that?'

The Doctor's smile faltered.

'The hands were dead before they hit the water,' he said sadly. Guiltily. 'But they didn't want to take any chances: they had the Loch filled in. Later on, they built the Princes Street Gardens on top. See that big spiky tower over there? That's the Scott Monument. That's where the Gardens are.'

Martha looked. She thought she could just see the belt of greenery at the foot of Castle Hill. Strange to think of all those little hands buried under there. She remembered what it had felt like when they'd all been raining down on her, scratching and choking her as she'd stood and held on. She looked around the hilltop: there were families there with little children, old couples sitting holding hands on the benches; a woman about Martha's age with bottle-blonde hair jumped down from the base of the Greek columns and went over on her ankle, laughing at her own clumsiness. Martha couldn't imagine what it would be like if the hands came back.

She remembered the walking dead, chasing the stagecoach through the Grassmarket. If it happened again now, the locals would probably think it was a stunt for some show or other, and tut to themselves about how much money the students had to waste.

'There's one thing I don't understand,' Martha said. The Doctor looked at her questioningly. 'The hands were broken, yes? They thought the dead bodies were that Kith thing, and they were just joining the rest of him? But they all still hung around together – the zombies didn't just wander off on their own.'

'The mechanism that made them combine had been damaged,' the Doctor said, a little guiltily. Martha could guess how it had been undamaged. 'But the psychic connection that made them group together was still there. That's why any damage Monro did with his electricity to the one hand managed to affect all the others under the Loch. They still wanted to find the other hands and join together. They just couldn't remember how.'

'So why was that first one chasing Benjamin Franklin?'

The Doctor nodded, looking back over the city.

'Only one reason I can think of,' he admitted quietly.

'He had a hand,' Martha said. Her heart beat a little harder.

'Probably the last one on Earth. They must have given it to him just before they packed him onto that stagecoach,' the Doctor said, still looking off into the distance. Was he remembering watching those hands fall into the Loch? He couldn't feel sorry for them, surely? 'All the others would have been destroyed by the lightning. Franklin's should have been safely on the way to London.'

'So he could clone himself?' Martha asked.

'Franklin?' the Doctor shook his head. 'I doubt it. The initial damage was a mistake. I don't think anybody but Monro could recreate it, and even then it would probably have taken him a good couple of years experimenting.'

'But Monro could do it?'

The Doctor shrugged casually.

'So shouldn't we be trying to get it back?' Martha suggested.

The Doctor spun around, his freshly laundered coat spinning with him. The smile was back on his face, the cheeky one that said he was going to suggest something particularly naughty. The one that Martha couldn't help but return, despite all her good arguments to the contrary.

'Martha Jones, your lack of knowledge about the history of medicine is truly shocking,' he mocked gently. 'Haven't you ever studied Edinburgh University's collection of Alexander Monros?'

She had to admit that she hadn't.

'Well, you can look it up next time we're near a library,' he said, stepping off with authority. 'In the meantime, why don't we go and try one of the local delicacies?'

'Haggis?' Martha wrinkled her nose.

The Doctor smiled.

'Chips,' he said, waggling his eyebrows. 'With salt and sauce.'

And they walked down Calton Hill arm in arm.

EDINBURGH, 1771

It had been a good long while since Ben Franklin had found himself in Edinburgh. With his duties in London and the two-week coach ride, it was very easy to put off coming to the city.

A lot had changed since he had last been here, with the work to build Craig's 'New Town' well under way. Ben wondered how the city would survive, splitting itself in twain like this, poor on one side and rich on the other. All those he had spoken to were optimistic, but then all those he had spoken to were also rich.

The door opened. Ben looked round to see his host, David Hume, entering the room.

'Your visitor from the University is here,' said Hume.

Ben looked uncomfortably at the ebony box sitting on the table beside him. Then he nodded to Hume.

'Show him in, please,' he said gently. 'And one other thing…'

'Don't worry, Ben,' Hume said. 'I'll leave you in peace for your spy-making.'

Ben nodded, and gently smiled as Hume left him alone again. The fire crackled nicely in the grate, and Ben looked at his cold ebony box and shivered.

The door opened, and the gentleman came in.

'Mr Franklin, thank you for coming,' he said without preamble.

'Your letter was insistent,' Ben said.

'You have it?' the gentleman asked. 'My father was keen to have your opinion on the… matter, given your expertise with electricity. But… well, my situation has changed recently, and it is time to reclaim the property. You do have it?'

Ben nodded to the box on the table.

'Don't worry,' he said. 'I have no qualms about giving it away. It is a strange specimen, and more than a little unnerving.'

The gentleman opened the box without comment, keen to check what was inside. Even in the gloom of the fire, Franklin could see the disembodied hand scuttle a little in its tiny prison. The gentleman smiled at it, clearly glad to have it back in his hands again.

'I was sorry to hear about your father's death,' Franklin said politely.

Alexander Monro smiled coldly.

'He is never truly gone so long as I am in the world,' he said.

And Ben Franklin shivered again.

Acknowledgements

My surprised gratitude to Justin Richards and Gary Russell for thinking kindly of the guy who wrote that one with the dolphin. Thanks also to Cathy Howkins, Nick Wallace, Mark Michalowski, Simon Forward and Jonn Elledge for all their help and suggestions throughout the writing process. Thanks to Mum, Dad, Darren, the Quibblers, the Copley-Robertses, the Channel Twelve collective, the Howkinses, Blade and my least attentive fan for their support, and to the kind Wikipedians who have helped keep my entry up to date.

Thanks to John Kendell and Glyn, who hopefully won't mind that I stole their names, and the kind people at St Cuthbert's, who hopefully won't mind that I stole their church. Thanks also to 'Aggie' from Mary King's Close for telling me lots of interesting things, including the bit about pantaloons.

And lastly, with respect and gratitude to the friends and family members who made up my supporting cast. In particular, thanks to the late Craig Hinton, who was in my thoughts whilst writing this and who would have been the first to congratulate me on my good fortune.

THE STONE ROSE
by Jacqueline Rayner

THE FEAST OF THE DROWNED
by Stephen Cole

THE RESURRECTION CASKET
by Justin Richards

THE NIGHTMARE OF BLACK ISLAND
by Mike Tucker

THE ART OF DESTRUCTION
by Stephen Cole

THE PRICE OF PARADISE
by Colin Brake

STING OF THE ZYGONS
by Stephen Cole

THE LAST DODO
by Jacqueline Rayner

WOODEN HEART
by Martin Day

FOREVER AUTUMN
by Mark Morris

SICK BUILDING
by Paul Magrs

WETWORLD
by Mark Michalowski

Also available from BBC Books
featuring the Doctor and Martha
as played by David Tennant and Freema Agyeman:

Sick Building

by Paul Magrs
ISBN 978 1 84607 269 7
UK £6.99 US $11.99/$14.99 CDN

Tiermann's World: a planet covered in wintry woods
and roamed by sabre-toothed tigers and other
savage beasts. The Doctor is here to warn Professor
Tiermann, his wife and their son that a terrible danger
is on its way.

The Tiermanns live in luxury, in a fantastic, futuristic,
fully automated Dreamhome, under an impenetrable
force shield. But that won't protect them from the
Voracious Craw. A gigantic and extremely hungry alien
creature is heading remorselessly towards their home.
When it gets there everything will be devoured.

Can they get away in time? With the force shield
cracking up, and the Dreamhome itself deciding who
should or should not leave, things are
looking desperate…

Also available from BBC Books
featuring the Doctor and Martha
as played by David Tennant and Freema Agyeman:

DOCTOR·WHO

Wetworld

by Mark Michalowski
ISBN 978 1 84607 271 0
UK £6.99 US $11.99/$14.99 CDN

When the TARDIS makes a disastrous landing in the
swamps of the planet Sunday, the Doctor has no choice
but to abandon Martha and try to find help. But the
tranquillity of Sunday's swamps is deceptive, and even
the TARDIS can't protect Martha forever.

The human pioneers of Sunday have their own dangers
to face: homeless and alone, they're only just starting to
realise that Sunday's wildlife isn't as harmless as it first
seems. Why are the native otters behaving so strangely,
and what is the creature in the swamps that is so
interested in the humans, and the new arrivals?

The Doctor and Martha must fight to ensure that
human intelligence doesn't become the greatest danger
of all.

Wishing Well

by Trevor Baxendale

ISBN 978 1 84607 348 9

UK £6.99 US $11.99/$14.99 CDN

The old village well is just a curiosity – something to attract tourists intrigued by stories of lost treasure, or visitors just making a wish. Unless something alien and terrifying could be lurking inside the well? Something utterly monstrous that causes nothing but death and destruction?

But who knows the real truth about the well? Who wishes to unleash the hideous force it contains? What terrible consequences will follow the search for a legendary treasure hidden at the bottom?

No one wants to believe the Doctor's warnings about the deadly horror lying in wait – but soon they'll wish they had…

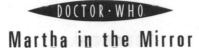
DOCTOR·WHO

Martha in the Mirror
by Justin Richards
ISBN 978 1 84607 420 2
UK £6.99 US $11.99/$14.99 CDN

Castle Extremis – whoever holds it can control
the provinces either side that have been at war for
centuries. Now the castle is about to play host to
the signing of a peace treaty. But as the Doctor
and Martha find out, not everyone wants the war
to end.

Who is the strange little girl who haunts the
castle? What is the secret of the book the Doctor
finds, its pages made from thin, brittle glass?
Who is the hooded figure that watches from the
shadows? And what is the secret of the legendary
Mortal Mirror?

The Doctor and Martha don't have long to find the
answers – an army is on the march, and the castle
will soon be under siege once more…

Coming soon from BBC Books:

DOCTOR · WHO

Starships and Spacestations

by Justin Richards

ISBN 978 1 84607 423 3

£7.99 US $12.99/$15.99 CDN

The Doctor has his TARDIS to get him from place to place and time to time, but the rest of the Universe relies on more conventional transport… From the British Space Programme of the late twentieth century to Earth's Empire in the far future, from the terrifying Dalek Fleet to deadly Cyber Ships, this book documents the many starships and spacestations that the Doctor and his companions have encountered on their travels.

He has been held prisoner in space, escaped from the moon, witnessed the arrival of the Sycorax and the crash landing of a space pig… More than anyone else, the Doctor has seen the development of space travel between countless worlds.

This stunningly illustrated book tells the amazing story of Earth's ventures into space, examines the many alien fleets who have paid Earth a visit, and explores the other starships and spacestations that the Doctor has encountered on his many travels…